Jenny bone

K-Son

D0648202

The Present

Johanna Lindsey

The Present

A MALORY HOLIDAY NOVEL

DOUBLEDAY DIRECT LARGE PRINT EDITION

Avon Books • New York

Avon Books, Inc.
1350 Avenue of the Americas
New York, New York 10019

Copyright © 1998 by Johanna Lindsey
Interior design by Kellan Peck
Visit our website at www.AvonBooks.com

ISBN: 0-7394-0121-1

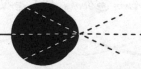

**This Large Print Book carries the
Seal of Approval of N.A.V.H.**

To the many fans
who love the Malorys as much as I do.
This present is for you.

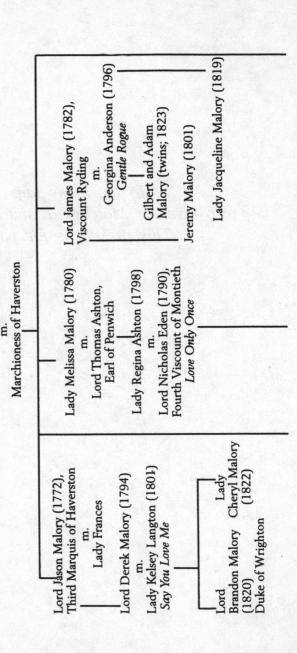

Malory Family Tree

Gypsy grandmother
The Second Marquis of Haverston
m.
Marchioness of Haverston

Lord Jason Malory (1772), Third Marquis of Haverston
m.
Lady Frances

Lord Derek Malory (1794)
m.
Lady Kelsey Langton (1801)
Say You Love Me

Lord Brandon Malory (1820) Duke of Wrighton

Lady Cheryl Malory (1822)

Lady Melissa Malory (1780)
m.
Lord Thomas Ashton, Earl of Penwich

Lady Regina Ashton (1798)
m.
Lord Nicholas Eden (1790), Fourth Viscount of Montieth
Love Only Once

Lord James Malory (1782), Viscount Ryding
m.
Georgina Anderson (1796)
Gentle Rogue

Gilbert and Adam Malory (twins; 1823)

Jeremy Malory (1801)

Lady Jacqueline Malory (1819)

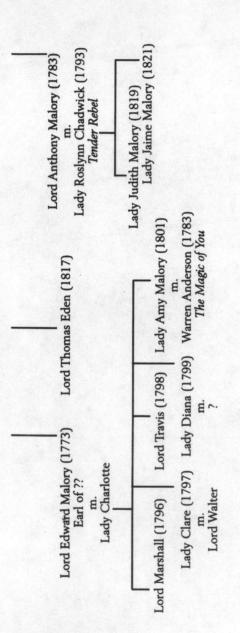

Lord Anthony Malory (1783)
m.
Lady Roslynn Chadwick (1793)
Tender Rebel

Lady Judith Malory (1819)
Lady Jaime Malory (1821)

Lord Thomas Eden (1817)

Lady Amy Malory (1801)
m.
Warren Anderson (1783)
The Magic of You

Lord Travis (1798)

Lady Diana (1799)
m.
?

Lord Edward Malory (1773)
Earl of ??
m.
Lady Charlotte

Lord Marshall (1796)

Lady Clare (1797)
m.
Lord Walter

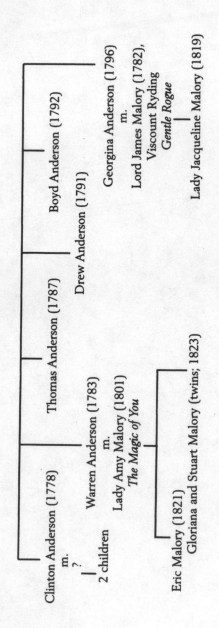

Anderson Family Tree

Clinton Anderson (1778)
m.
?
2 children

Warren Anderson (1783)
m.
Lady Amy Malory (1801)
The Magic of You

Thomas Anderson (1787)

Drew Anderson (1791)

Boyd Anderson (1792)

Georgina Anderson (1796)
m.
Lord James Malory (1782),
Viscount Ryding
Gentle Rogue

Eric Malory (1821)

Gloriana and Stuart Malory (twins; 1823)

Lady Jacqueline Malory (1819)

The Present

Chapter One

England, 1825

The Malory clan always spent the Christmas holidays at Haverston, the ancestral estate in the country where the oldest among them had been born and raised. Jason Malory, Third Marquis of Haverston and the oldest of four brothers, was the only family member who was still a permanent resident. The head of the family since he was only sixteen, Jason had raised his brothers—two of whom had been utterly scandalous in their pursuits—and a young sister.

At present the various Malorys and offspring were quite numerous and difficult to place, sometimes even for Jason himself. So it was a very large brood that gathered at Haverston these days for the Christmas season.

Jason's only son and heir, Derek, was the first to arrive, more than a week before Christmas. With him came his wife, Kelsey, and Jason's first two blond and green-eyed grandchildren.

Anthony, his youngest brother, was the next to arrive only a few days after Derek. Tony, as most of the family called him, admitted to Jason that he'd deserted London early after hearing that their brother James had a bone to pick with him. Annoying James was one thing, and something Anthony often strived to do, but when James was out for blood, well, Tony considered that a different matter entirely.

Anthony and James were his youngest brothers, yet only a year apart in age themselves. They were both skilled pugilists, and Anthony could hold his own with the best of them, yet James was heftier, and his fists were frequently likened to solid bricks.

With Anthony came his wife, Roslynn, and their two daughters. Judith, the oldest at six, had taken after both her parents, having her mother's glorious red-gold hair and her father's cobalt blue eyes, a seriously striking combination that Anthony feared was going to make her the reigning beauty of her day—which as her father and a reformed rake he was *not* looking forward to.

But his younger daughter, Jaime, was going to break some hearts as well.

But even with all his guests, Jason was the first one to notice the present that had appeared in the parlor while the family was breakfasting. It was hard to miss, actually, placed prominently up on a pedestal table next to the fireplace. Wrapped in gold cloth, banded with a red velvet ribbon and bow, it was oddly shaped, nearly like the size of a thick book, yet a round protrusion on top suggested it was nothing that simple.

Poking a finger at it showed that the protrusion could move, yet not very much, as he found out when he tilted the present sideways and it didn't change position. Strange, yet stranger still was that there was no indication of whom the present was from, nor whom it was for.

"A bit early to be passing out Christmas gifts, ain't it?" Anthony remarked as he sauntered into the room to find Jason holding the present. "The Christmas tree ain't even been brought in yet."

"That was my thought as well, since I didn't put it here," Jason replied.

"No? Then who?"

"I've no idea," Jason admitted.

"Who's it for, then?" Anthony asked.

"I'd like to know that myself."

Anthony raised a brow at that point. "No card?"

Jason shook his head. "None. I just found it here on this pedestal myself," he said, and put it back.

Anthony picked up the present as well to poke at it a bit. "Hmmm, someone sure dressed it up fancy. I'll wager it will fascinate the children—at least until we find out what it is."

As it happened, it fascinated the adults as well. In the following days, since none of the family owned up to having put it there, the present created a sensation. Just about all of the adults poked, shook, or otherwise examined it, yet no one could figure out what it might be, or whom it was for.

Those having arrived so far were gathered in the parlor the night when Amy walked in holding one of her twins. "Don't ask why we're late, you wouldn't believe it," she said, then in the next breath, "First the wheel on the coach fell off. Then not a mile down the road, one of the horses lost not one, but two of his shoes. After we finally get that all taken care of and we're almost here, the bloody axle broke. I thought surely Warren was going to kill that poor coach by then. He certainly kicked it enough. If I didn't think to wager with him that we *would* arrive here today, I really don't think we would have. But you know I never lose a wager, so . . . By the by, Uncle Jason, what's an unmarked grave doing in that lovely clearing east of here? The one close to the road that runs through your property? We ended up walking through it to get here, since it was the shorter route by that point, to just head across that clearing."

No one said a word at first, still in bemusement after that long dissertation. But then Derek said, "Remember that grave m'self, now that you mention it, cousin. Reggie and I came across it when we were younguns gadding about the estate. Always meant to ask you about it, Father, just never got around to it, then forgot about it."

They were all looking toward Jason by then, but he merely shrugged his broad shoulders. "Devil if I know who was laid to rest there. That grave has been there since before I was born. Asked my father about it once, as I recall, but he put off answering, hemmed and hawed so much, actually, that I figured he just didn't know, so I didn't ask again."

"Think we've all come across that grave at one time or another, least those of us who were raised here," Anthony remarked to no one in particular. "Strange place for a grave, and a well-tended one at that, when there are two cemeteries nearby, not to mention the ancestral cemetery right here on the property."

Judith, who had been standing next to the pedestal staring at the mysterious present, came over to her cousin Amy and held up her arms to take the two-year-old twin from her. Judy was tall for her age, and very good with the toddlers. Amy was only surprised that she got no greeting, and said so.

"Where's my hug, puss?"

Those exquisite features just stared at her mulishly. Amy raised a brow toward the girl's father.

Anthony rolled his eyes, but explained, "She's pouting 'cause Jack ain't here yet."

Jack was James and Georgina's oldest daughter. Everyone knew that Jack and Judy, who were only months apart in age, were inseparable when they were together, and they were so fond of each other that their parents made sure they were often together—especially since neither was very happy when they were separated for very long.

"Am not," Judith denied in a pouting mumble as she marched back to the pedestal.

Jason was the only one to notice when Amy's attention centered on the present that had garnered everyone's curiosity. He would have thought nothing of it, except for her expression. Her brief frown made him wonder if she was getting one of her feelings about it. This niece of his had phenomenal luck, never having lost a wager in her life, which she attributed to these "feelings," as she called them, that she got. Jason considered such things as feelings exceeding strange, which was why he would as soon not hear if she was getting one now. So he was relieved when her frown eased and she gave her attention back to his brother.

"Uncle James hasn't arrived yet, then?" Amy surmised from Anthony's last response.

Anthony did some mumbling himself. "No, and hopefully he won't."

"Oh, dear. You two are fighting?" Amy surmised again.

"Me? Fight my dear brother? Wouldn't think of it," Anthony replied, then, "But someone bloody well ought to tell him this is the season for good cheer."

Derek chuckled at his uncle's sour expression. "Heard a rumor Uncle James was out for your hide. What's set him off this time?"

"If I knew, then I'd know how to defuse him, but I'm deuced if I know. Ain't seen James for a good week, not since I dropped off Jack after the outing I took the girls on."

"Well, James would have let me know if he wasn't coming," Jason pointed out. "So when he gets here, kindly take any altercations outside. Molly seriously objects to blood staining the carpets."

No one would think it strange that he called Haverston's housekeeper by her first name. After all, Molly Fletcher had held that position for more than twenty years. That she was also Jason's very longtime mistress—and Derek's mother—was not something that everyone in the family was aware of, however. In fact, only a couple of members had ever learned or guessed the truth. Jason had only told Derek, his son, about this time six years ago.

And around that Christmas, Jason, who deplored all scandals attached to the family, was willing to create one in giving his wife, Frances, the divorce she wanted, just to keep her from revealing what she knew about Molly.

But since then, Molly had remained the housekeeper. Jason had tried, ever since Derek found out the truth, to get her to marry him, but she was still refusing.

Molly didn't come from gentry. She had in fact been just a parlor maid when she and Jason fell in love more'n thirty years ago. And although he was willing to make one of the worse scandals possible, that of an esteemed lord marrying a commoner, she wasn't willing to let him.

Jason sighed, thinking of it. He had been forced to come to the conclusion that she would never give him the answer he so wanted to hear. Which didn't mean he was giving up, not by any means.

He was drawn back to the conversation when Amy said, "There is a little idiosyncrasy our twins have developed. Strangest behavior. When Stuart wants Warren's attention, I might as well be a stranger to him, he ignores me so thoroughly, and vice versa, when he wants my attention, Warren can't do a thing with him. And Glory does the same thing exactly."

"Least they do it at the same time," Warren, who had finally arrived, added as he reached for Stuart and handed Gloriana to Amy.

"I've been meaning to ask Uncle James and Aunt George if they're having the same problem with theirs," Amy said with a sigh.

"Has he gotten used to them yet?" Jason asked Anthony, since Anthony, being closest to James, saw him the most often, and Jason didn't get to London often.

"Course he has," Anthony assured the family.

Yet they all still remembered his reaction when Amy had borne twins and he'd asked his wife Georgina, who was Warren's sister, where they came from. "Good God, George, you could have warned me that twins run in your family every other generation. We are *not* having any, d'you hear!"

Georgina had been pregnant again herself at the time, and had given birth to just that, twin boys.

Yes, the Malorys at Christmas were a wonderful sight, Jason thought. His life only lacked one thing to make it perfection.

Chapter Two

As the housekeeper, Molly usually wasn't present when the Malorys dined, but today she was supervising a new maid who was serving for the first time. By long practice, she managed to keep her eyes away from Jason's handsome face, sitting at the head of the table. It wasn't that she thought she might give herself away if she was caught staring at him, though she supposed that was a distinct possibility. Sometimes she simply couldn't keep her feelings from showing, and she had a lot of feelings where Jason Malory was concerned.

No, she wasn't so much worried that she might give herself away, it was that lately, *he* was revealing too much when he looked at her, and he didn't seem to care anymore who might notice. And with the house rapidly filling up with his entire family, there were a lot more people around who just might notice.

Molly was beginning to suspect that he was doing it on purpose, that he was hoping they would be found out. Not that it would change her mind about anything, but he might think it would.

It wouldn't, and she was going to have to assure him of that if he didn't return to his usual show of indifference when others were around. They had always been so careful, never giving away by look, word, or deed what they meant to each other, at least when they weren't alone. Until their son learned the truth, the only one who had ever come upon them in a moment of intimacy had been Jason's niece Amy, when she'd caught them kissing. And that wouldn't have happened if Jason hadn't been foxed at the time.

Keeping their relationship a secret had always been important to her. She wasn't gentry, after all, and she loved Jason too much to cause him embarrassment. Her lack of social status was also why she had convinced Jason that Derek should never know either, that she was his mother, though he hadn't wanted to keep that from his son. Not that Jason had considered marrying her back then. But he'd been young and, like anyone else of his class, adhered to the fact that a lord did not marry his lowborn mistress.

He had instead married an earl's daughter, just to give Derek and his niece Reggie a mother figure. Which had ended up a disastrous decision, since his wife, Frances, had been anything but maternal. A pale, thin woman, Frances hadn't wanted to marry Jason in the first place, had been forced to it by her father. She'd deplored his touch, and their marriage had never even been consummated. She had lived most of it separated from him, and had finally insisted on a divorce, which she had ultimately used blackmail to obtain.

Frances had been the only other member of the family to figure out that Molly was Jason's mistress and Derek's mother, and she had threatened to tell Derek this if Jason didn't end their marriage. The family had weathered that scandal fairly well, and six years later, it was rarely if ever mentioned anymore. Jason could have stopped it—Derek had actually learned the truth before the scandal of the divorce reached the gossip mills—yet he hadn't.

"This is something that should have been done years ago," he had told her at the time. "Actually, it's a marriage that never should have been. But then it's rarely easy, to correct the mistakes one makes in one's youth."

The reasons he had made the match had been good ones. The reasons he had ended it were good ones, too. But ever since it was ended, he'd been asking Molly to marry him, to her utter frustration, when he knew she'd never agree. And her reasons were no different than they'd ever been. She was *not* going to be the cause of yet another Malory scandal. She hadn't been raised that way. And besides she was already more a wife to him than Frances had ever been.

But she knew that her continued refusals to marry him, or even let him tell the rest of his family about their love, had been frustrating him as well for a very long time. Which was why she was afraid he was hoping the matter would come to light inadvertently. Not that he was being blatant in looks he was giving her, nothing the servants might take note of, at any rate. Yet his family was different. They knew him too well. And they would *all* be here soon . . .

More arrived even as Molly had the thought. Jason's niece Reggie and her husband, Nicholas, along with their young son, appeared in the dining room before lunch was finished. Anthony perked up immediately. Reggie might have been his favorite niece, but that didn't save her husband. Nicholas was his favorite verbal punching bag, so to speak, and without the presence of his brother James, whom he would just as soon trade barbs with, he'd been sorely missing a convenient target for his satirical wit.

Molly just managed to refrain from rolling her eyes. She knew Jason's family as well as he did, since he shared everything with her, including all the family secrets, foibles, and scandals.

So she wasn't the least bit surprised to hear Anthony say to Nicholas as he took the seat across from him, "Good of you to show up, dear boy. My teeth were getting a tad dull."

"Old age starting to set in, is it?" Nick shot back with a smirk.

Molly noticed the nudge Anthony's wife gave him before she said, "Remember it's Christmas and be nice for a change."

Up went Anthony's black brow. "For a change? I'm always nice. There's just nice, and then there's—nice. The latter gets reserved for bounders like Eden, is all."

Molly sighed. As fond as she was of all of Jason's family, she had a soft spot for Nicholas Eden, because he had befriended her son in their school days, when Derek had had to deal with his public illegitimacy. He and Derek had been close friends ever since. And typically, Derek jumped in now to take Anthony's attention off of Nick.

"Reggie, you remember that grave we found in the east clearing all those years ago?" Derek said to his cousin. "As I recall, you were going to ask one of the gardeners about it. Did you ever get around to doing that?"

Reggie gave him an owlish look. "Goodness, what made you think of that old grave? It's been so long since we found it, I'd forgotten all about it."

"Amy came across it last night and mentioned it. M'father don't even know who it belongs to."

Reggie peered at her cousin Amy. "What were you doing in that clearing last night?"

"Don't ask," Amy mumbled.

And Warren, obviously finding their catastrophes of the day before rather amusing now, after the fact, said, "A little coach trouble."

"A little!" Amy snorted indelicately. "That coach is cursed, I tell you. Who did you say you bought it from, Warren? Because you were definitely swindled."

He chuckled and patted her hand. "Don't worry about it, sweetheart. I'm sure the crew I sent over to dismantle it this morning will make good use of the kindling."

Amy nodded, then turned back to her cousin. "We ended up having to cross that clearing on foot last night. It just surprised me, to find a grave there, so far from the family plots, yet still on the property."

"Now that you mention it, it surprised Derek and me, too, when we found it all those years ago," Reggie replied thoughtfully. "But no, Derek, I don't believe I did ever get around to asking the gardeners. It's too far from the gardens, after all. Figured whoever was tending it probably didn't live at Haverston, so it wouldn't do much good to ask around."

"Unless one of the gardeners was specifically asked to tend it," Anthony pointed out. "Old John Markus was ancient when I still lived here, and he'd worked at Haverston for as long as anyone could remember. If anyone might know about that grave, it would be him. Don't suppose he'd still be around, would he, Jason?"

Like everyone else, Molly glanced toward Jason to hear his answer, and caught his tender expression on her. Her checks went up in flames. He'd done it! She couldn't believe he'd done it! And with half his family here to see it. But she was panicking for nothing. The look he'd given her had been brief, and no one was turning about to see who he'd been looking at, too interested in his answer, which he gave now.

"Here at Haverston, no," Jason replied. "He retired about fifteen years ago. But he's still alive, last I heard. Living with a daughter over in Havers Town."

"Think I'll ride over and pay my respects to Mr. Markus this afternoon," Derek said.

"I'll go with you," Reggie offered. "I've a few Christmas presents I still have to buy, so I was going to stop by Havers anyway."

Warren shook his head in bemusement. "I don't understand all this morbid curiosity about an old grave. It's obviously not someone in the family, or the grave would be in the family crypt."

"I suppose you'd think nothing of it if someone got buried in your backyard, and no one bothered to tell you who it was or why they picked your backyard?" Anthony asked. "Perfectly normal occurrence in America, is it, Yank, having unmarked graves show up on your properties?"

"I would imagine someone was asked and did know—at the time," Warren replied. "Or the grave would probably have been removed to a more proper location—at the time. And it seems pretty obvious that the grave is older than any of you, since none of you know when it got there or who's in it."

"Well, that's what I object to," Reggie put in. "It's just too sad, really, that whoever it was has been so completely forgotten. At the very least, her name should be added to that stone marker that merely says 'SHE RESTS.' "

"Think I'll join you as well for that jaunt to Havers," Amy said. "I was going to help Molly fetch the rest of the Christmas decorations from the attic this afternoon, but that can wait until tonight."

Molly was sure she'd learn later, whatever they found out in Havers Town, but right now she really couldn't care less. With her cheeks still heated, she slipped out of the room unnoticed. And it was already going through her mind, what she was going to say to Jason when she got him alone tonight.

That had been too close by half. If his relatives hadn't all been so interested in the subject at hand, at least one of them would have noticed the way he had looked at her. And that would be the end of their secret.

But what good would it do? It still wouldn't change her mind about marrying him, though that was something she wished she could do, with all her heart. But one of them had to remain sensible about this. Even if he did marry her, she'd never be accepted by the ton. She'd be nothing but another Malory scandal.

Chapter Three

As it happened, the trip to Havers Town turned out to be utterly unsatisfactory. John Markus was indeed still living at the advanced age of ninety-six. He was bed-ridden, yet his mind was quite lively for his age, and he did indeed recall the grave.

"I tended that grave for nigh on sixty-eight years," John proudly told the group gathered about his bed.

"Goodness!" Reggie exclaimed. "That's long before even you were born, Uncle Jason."

"Aye." John nodded. "Since I was a lad of thirteen myself. Turned the task over to my nephew when I retired fifteen years ago. Wouldn't trust anyone else to do it proper. He ain't been slacking, has he?"

"No, John, of course not," Jason assured him, though he hadn't a clue, since he hadn't been out to see that grave in over thirty years himself. But he didn't want the old man worrying about it, so he added, "He's been doing an excellent job, indeed he has."

"We're delighted to have found someone who knows about that grave, Mr. Markus," Reggie told him, getting to the matter that had brought them there in mass. "It's been a point of curiosity for all of us, to know who is buried there."

The old man frowned. "Who is? Well now, I don't rightly know that."

The surprised silence that followed that answer was full of disappointment. It was Derek who finally asked, "Then why did you keep care of it all those years?"

"Because she asked me to."

"She?" Jason inquired.

"Why, your grandma, Lord Jason. Wasn't anything I wouldn't have done for that kind lady. Everyone at Haverston felt that way. She was well loved, your grandma was—not like your grandpa. Or at least not as he was regarded when he was young."

Up went a half dozen brows, but it was Jason who said indignantly, "I beg your pardon?"

The old man chuckled, too old to be intimidated by Jason Malory's ire. "No disrespect intended, m'lord, but the first marquis, he was a stiff one, though no different from other aristocrats of his day. He was given Haverston by the crown, but he had little care for it or its people. He preferred London, and came only once a year for an accounting by his estate agent, who was an arrogant coxcomb that ruled Haverston like a tyrant when the marquis wasn't there."

"A rather harsh testament against a man who can't defend himself," Jason said stiffly.

John shrugged thin shoulders before saying, "Merely the truth as I saw it, but that was before the marquis met and married Lady Anna. She changed him, she did, taught him to appreciate the little things in life, softened his edges. Haverston went from being a dismal, bleak place to work, to being a place her people took pride in calling home. A real shame about the rumors, though . . ."

"Rumors?" Reggie frowned. "Oh, you mean about her being a Gypsy?"

"Aye, that one. Just because she looked and sounded foreign, and there happened to have been Gypsies in the area just before her appearance, some folks got that silly notion. But the marquis, he put a stop to that rumor when he married her. After all, a lord like him would never marry so far beneath him, now would he?"

Jason intercepted his son's grin just before Derek remarked, "Depends on the lord."

Jason gave him a quelling look. The rest of the family didn't need to know—yet—that he, too, hoped to put his heart first.

John shook his head. "Back then it just wasn't done, Lord Derek. Today, maybe, but eighty-some years ago, a scandal like that would ruin a man."

"Well, rumor was all it ever was," Jason pointed out, "since it's never been proven, one way or the other. The rumor wasn't completely put to rest, though, or it wouldn't still be known. But as you say, it hardly matters in this day and age, whether Anna Malory was Gypsy or of Spanish descent, as most assumed. Only she could answer that, but my grandparents died before I was born. I'm sorry I never knew them."

"I've always wished to know the truth about her myself," Amy said. "I can remember being fascinated by the possibility when I was a child, and before you ask why again, recall that I take after her, or so I've been told. I wanted to think she really was a Gypsy—I still wish it was so. That would at least explain where I got such unusually perceptive instincts from, that are never wrong. And it must have been true love."

"Hell, if it's true love, I'm glad our ancestor realized it," Derek put in. "For some men, it takes years . . . and years . . . and—"

Jason didn't miss the subtle prodding directed his way, but before anyone else noticed, he said pointedly, "Didn't you say you had a bit of shopping to do while we were in town, Derek?" To which his son just grinned again, unrepentantly.

Jason sighed inwardly. He knew Derek was just teasing him. Actually, Derek was the only one in the family who ever dared tease him. And no one else, being aware of who Molly really was, would guess that he *was* teasing his father. But then Derek knew that Jason had been after Molly for a long time now to say yes to marrying him.

"Hmmm, wonder why I never thought to do that with Anna Malory," Amy remarked to herself, drawing everyone's attention again.

"Do what?" more than one Malory asked in unison.

"Make a bet that we'd learn the truth about her. Anyone care to take up the wager?"

But Jason interrupted with, "I'd prefer this speculation ended here."

Amy frowned. "You really don't want to know the truth, Uncle Jason?"

"I didn't say that, m'dear. I just don't want to see you break your perfect win record on something that can't possibly come to light. You would be devastated if that happened, now wouldn't you?"

Her sigh answered him, but didn't quite reassure him. After all, he was well aware that horrible odds had never stopped her from following her instincts in the past.

Chapter Four

The family was spread out in the large country mansion that evening after dinner. Molly had carefully unpacked most of the Christmas paraphernalia from the attic earlier in the week, and it was Molly, just reaching the bottom of the stairs, who heard the horse come to a galloping halt out front and went to see who was visiting this late in the evening. Just as she reached to open the door, it was opened from without and Jason's brother James nearly knocked her over as he stomped in out of the cold.

Nonetheless, she was delighted to see he had arrived at last, even at that late hour, and offered a cheery, "Merry Christmas, Ja—"

To which he immediately cut her off with

a very testy, "Bloody hell it is." Though he did halt his progress to offer her a brief smile, adding, "Good to see you, Molly," then in the same breath, "Where's that worthless brother of mine?"

She was surprised enough to ask, "Ah, which brother would that be?" when she knew very well he would never refer to Edward or Jason, whom the two younger brothers termed the elders, in that way. But then, Jason shared everything with her about his family, so she knew them as well as he did.

So his derogatory answer didn't really add to her surprise. "The infant."

She winced at his tone, though, as well as his expression, which had reverted to deadly menace at mention of the "infant." Big, blond, and handsome, James Malory was, just like his elder brothers, and rarely did anyone actually see him *looking* angry. When James was annoyed with someone, he usually very calmly ripped the person to shreds with his devilish wit, and by his inscrutable expression, the victim had absolutely no warning such pointed barbs would be headed his or her way.

The infant, or rather, Anthony, had heard James's voice and, unfortunately, stuck his head around the parlor door to determine James's mood, which wasn't hard to mis-interpret with the baleful glare that came his way. Which was probably why the parlor door immediately slammed shut.

"Oh, dear," Molly said as James stormed off. Through the years she'd be-come accustomed to the Malorys' behav-ior, but at times it still alarmed her.

What ensued was a tug of war in the reverse, so to speak, with James shoving his considerable weight against the parlor door, and Anthony on the other side doing his best to keep it from opening. Anthony managed for a bit. He wasn't as hefty as his brother, but he was taller and well mus-cled. But he must have known he couldn't hold out indefinitely, especially when James started to slam his shoulder against the door, which got it nearly half open before Anthony could manage to slam it shut again.

But what Anthony did to solve his di-lemma produced Molly's second "Oh, dear."

When James threw his weight against the door for the third time, it opened ahead of him and he unfortunately couldn't halt his progress into the room. A rather loud crash followed. A few moments later James was up again dusting pine needles off his shoulders.

Reggie and Molly, alarmed by the noise, soon followed the men into the room.

Anthony had picked up his daughter Jaime who had been looking at the tree with her nursemaid and was now holding her like a shield in front of him while the tree lay ingloriously on its side. Anthony knew his brother wouldn't risk harming one of the children for any reason, and the ploy worked.

"Infants hiding behind infants, how apropos," James sneered.

"Is, ain't it?" Anthony grinned and kissed the top of his daughter's head. "Least it works."

James was not amused, and ordered, barked, actually, "Put my niece down."

"Wouldn't think of it, old man—least not until I find out why you want to murder me."

Anthony's wife, Roslynn, bent over one

of the twins, didn't turn about to say, "Excuse me? There will be no murdering in front of the children."

The smirk that elicited from Anthony had James raising a golden brow at him. That, of course, gave Anthony ample warning that he wouldn't like what was coming, knowing his brother as he did.

And James didn't keep him in suspense, saying, "Ask yourself what would happen when Jack, out of the blue, mutters, 'bloody everlasting hell,' within her mother's hearing. Then ask yourself what would happen when George asks her daughter where she heard such a phrase. Then imagine what would happen when Jack, unaware that she had just shocked her mother, pipes up that Uncle Tony took Judy and her to Knighton's Hall. Finally, imagine George hunting me down to demand why I *let* you take our daughters to that strictly male establishment where blood flies freely in the ring, where gamblers swear most foully when they lose their wagers on the contenders who get too bloody, where every kind of topic unsuitable for six-year-olds gets discussed freely.

And *then* picture George not believing me when I tell her that I didn't know you could be that bloody irresponsible. She blamed me for letting you take them there. And since I didn't even *know* you were taking them there, guess who I'm bloody well blaming?"

Even Reggie took a deep breath after that long diatribe. Anthony had looked rather shocked at first, but now he looked quite uncomfortable, especially when his wife turned to narrow her gold-flecked hazel eyes on him, her Scots temper obviously about to erupt.

"Och, mon, I canna believe what I just heard. You did that? You actually took Judy and Jack to Knighton's, of all places? You didna ken how damaging that could be to such impressionable young girls?"

Anthony winced and tried quickly to explain. "It wasn't like that, Ros, really it wasn't. I was taking the girls to the park. I stopped by Knighton's just to run in quickly to have a word with Amherst. You had asked me to invite him and Frances to dinner, and I knew he'd be at Knighton's Hall at that time of day. How was I to guess the girls would sneak out of the carriage and follow me in?"

"When those two darlings are known to be getting into things and places they shouldna?" she retorted stiffly, then turned to Reggie. "Fetch the other two bairns," she said as she scooped up the twins. "We're leaving James to get on with his murdering."

Reggie tried to hide her grin as she plucked Jaime from Anthony and grabbed the other toddler's hand, then followed Roslynn out of the room. It was accomplished within moments, as efficient as the women were with children.

James leaned back against the door after it closed, crossed his arms over his exceedingly wide chest, and said to his bemused brother, "How's it feel, old chap? Least she was still talking to you before she flounced out of here, whereas George ain't talked to me in a week."

"Bloody hell," Anthony growled. "*You* can stop blaming me. You heard what I said. Wasn't as if I deliberately took the girls to Knighton's. Same thing could have happened to you, you know."

"Beg to differ," James replied laconically. "I ain't that bloody stupid."

Anthony flushed angrily, but it was a bit of guilt that had him retorting, "I like that. You want a piece of me, then? Won't be satisfied without it? Have at me, then."

"Don't mind if I do."

Chapter Five

The problems that arose with the staff with so many guests in the house were typically wearing on Molly, who prided herself on keeping everything running smoothly. So though she wanted to confront Jason about her suspicions, she'd been unable to stay awake long enough last night to wait for him to come to her room.

But he had joined her as usual, and he was still there in her bed when she awoke the next morning. In fact, it was his hand gently caressing her breast and his lips on the side of her neck that woke her. And although she did recall near immediately that she was annoyed with him, she selfishly kept that to herself for the moment and instead turned slightly so that he could better reach the areas of her body that he was showing an interest in.

She sighed and put her arms around him. She did so love this man. Even after more than thirty years, his touch still thrilled her beyond measure, his kisses able to fire her passions just as easily as he'd done in their youth. And she knew she had the same effect on him.

It wasn't long before they were kissing quite heatedly, and Molly knew where that would lead, which it did. But she was ready for him. She was always ready for him. She supposed that was one of the nicer benefits of loving someone and desiring him as well. And Jason never stinted in his endeavors. His lovemaking was done in no small measure and immensely satisfying— as always.

"Good morning," he said, leaning back to grin at her once they both regained their composure.

A morning could easily go sour, but he sure knew how to start one off "good." She returned his grin and then held him extra tight before she released him, perhaps because she knew she was going to scold before they parted, and she wanted to soften the blow.

The rest of his family, aside from their son, saw him as the sternest of the lot, even quite formidable. He was, after all, the head of his family and had had the responsibility of raising his younger siblings when he'd been young himself. But she knew his other side, his charm, his teasing, his tenderness. These were things that, from habit, he restrained in front of others due to his position, but not with her, never with her—except, of course, when they weren't alone.

That was the rub that was frustrating him, and yet she could see no way around it. He wanted to treat her at all times as he did when they were alone, yet he had to marry her to do so, and she wouldn't let him. And his insisting that they marry and her continued refusal was putting a strain on their relationship. One of them was going to have to give in, and as far as Molly was concerned, it wasn't going to be her.

She was nearly dressed before she put a damper on *his* morning with what she had to say, but it had to be said. "Do I need to hide from you in the day, Jason, while your family is here?"

He sat up more fully in the bed, where he had been lazily watching her as she went about her morning toilet. "Where did that question come from?"

"From the way you were looking at me yesterday in the dining room, which anyone there could have noticed. This isn't the first time. What has gotten into you, that you so forget that I'm merely your house-keeper?"

"The fact that you *aren't* merely my housekeeper?" he countered, but then sighed, admitting, "I think it's this time of year, Molly. I can't help but recall that it was at Christmas that Derek overcame Kelsey's objections to marrying him, and her reasons had been the same as yours."

She was surprised to hear that, that the very season was making him brood about it, and was quick to point out, "But there's a huge difference and you know it. Good God, Jason, she descends from a duke. Anyone can be forgiven with such an illustrious family as hers. Besides, the scandal she feared was avoided completely. *Yours* wouldn't be."

"How many times do I have to assure you that I don't care anymore? I want you for my wife, Molly. I obtained a special license to marry you years ago. All you have to do is say yes and we could be married today."

"Oh, Jason, you're going to make me cry," she said sadly. "You know I'd like nothing better. But one of us has to consider the consequences, and since you won't, I must. And letting your family know, which you seem to be trying to do inadvertently, won't change anything, it will merely embarrass me horribly. I have a measure of respect in this household. I will have none if it becomes common knowledge that I'm your mistress."

He came to her then, completely naked as he still was and without a thought for it, to draw her into his arms. She heard his sigh before he said, "You don't think with your heart enough."

"And you don't think with your mind enough—lately," she rejoined.

He leaned back to give her a wry smile. "Well, we can agree on that at least."

Her hand rose to caress his cheek. "Jason, let it go, it can never happen. I'm sorry that my birth was common. I'm sorry that your peers would never accept me as one of their members, whether you marry me or not. I can't change any of that. I can only continue to love you and try to make you happy as best I can. You have to let it go."

"You know I'll never accept that," was his stubborn and not unexpected reply.

She sighed now. "I know."

"But I'll make the effort you want and *try* to ignore you during the day—at least when my family is around."

She almost laughed. It was damned hard, getting him to concede anything these days, at least on this subject. She supposed she was going to have to take what she could get—for now.

Chapter Six

When James entered the breakfast room that morning, it was to varied reactions. Those who hadn't known that he'd arrived started cheerful greetings that sputtered to an end as they got a good look at his face. Those who did know of his arrival and what subsequently followed it were either tactfully silent, grinning from ear to ear, or foolish enough to remark on it.

Jeremy fell into the middle and latter categories when he said with a chuckle, "Well, I know the poor Christmas tree didn't do that to you, though you did try valiantly to chop it down to size."

"And succeeded, as I recall," James grouched, though he did think to ask, "Was it salvageable, puppy?"

"Minus a few of its feathers is all, but

those pretty little candles will dress it up so as not to notice—at least if someone other than me finishes the task. I'm much better at hanging the mistletoe."

"And making good use of it," Amy noted with a fond smile for her handsome cousin.

Jeremy winked at her. "That goes without saying."

Jeremy had turned twenty-five not too long ago and had turned out to be a charming scamp. Ironically, he so resembled his Uncle Anthony that he was nearly a mirror image of Anthony in his younger years. But then rather than taking after his own father, Jeremy had gained the cobalt blue eyes and black hair that only a few of the Malorys had possessed, those who took after the ancestor rumored to have been a Gypsy.

The mention of mistletoe and the use it was most noted for put James back into his sour mood, because he knew he wouldn't be doing any kissing under the festive greenery this year himself, not with his wife refusing to come to Haverston with him because of *her* sour mood. Bloody hell.

He would get this settled between them, one way or another. Taking his frustration with the situation out on Anthony hadn't helped—well, perhaps it had a little.

Warren, still staring at the splendid black eye and several cuts on his face, remarked, "Hate to see what the other fellow looks like," which James supposed was a compliment of sorts, since Warren had personal experience of his fists from numerous occasions himself.

"Like to congratulate the other fellow myself," Nicholas said with a smirk, which got him a kick under the table from his wife.

James nodded to Reggie. "Appreciate it, m'dear. My feet wouldn't reach."

To which she blushed that her kick had been noticed. And Nicholas, still wincing, managed a scowl, which turned out rather comical looking, considering the two expressions didn't mix all that well.

"Is Uncle Tony still among the living?" Amy asked, probably because neither James or his brother had returned back downstairs last night.

"Give me a few more days to figure that out, puss, 'cause I bloody well ain't sure just now," Anthony said as he came slowly into the room, an arm tucked to his side as if he were protecting some broken ribs.

A melodramatic groan escaped as he took the seat across from his brother. James rolled his eyes hearing it.

"Give over, you ass," he sneered. "Your wife ain't here to witness your theatrics."

"She's not?" Anthony glanced down the table, then made a moue and sat back in his chair—minus any groaning this time. However, he did complain to James, "You *did* break my ribs, you know."

"Devil I did, though I'll admit I considered it. And by the by, the option is still open."

Anthony glared at him. "We're too bloody old to be beating on each other."

"Speak for yourself, old man. One is never too old for a spot of exercise."

"Ah, so that's what we were doing?" Anthony shot back dryly, as he gently fingered his own black eye. "Exercising, was it?"

James raised a brow. "And that's not what you do weekly at Knighton's Hall? But I understand your confusion in the matter, since you're used to doling out the damage, rather than receiving any. Tends to give one a skewed perspective. Glad to have cleared that up for you."

It was at that point that Jason walked in, took one look at his two younger brothers' battered faces, and remarked, "Good God, and at this time of the year, no less? I'll see you both in my study."

That Jason said it in that not-to-be-disobeyed tone that he was renowned for, and promptly exited the room again, left little doubt, in James and Anthony's mind at least, that they were to follow immediately. James rose without expression and came around the table.

Anthony, however, huffed in annoyance, "Called on the carpet at our age? I bloody well don't believe it. And I won't forget who instigated—"

"Oh, put a lid on it, puppy," James said as he dragged Anthony out of the room with him. "It's been so long since we've had the pleasure of seeing Jason rant and rave, I'm looking forward to this myself."

"You would," Anthony replied in disgust. "You always did enjoy provoking his rages."

James grinned unrepentantly. "I did, didn't I? Well, what can I say? The elder is just so amusing when he flies through the roof."

"Well, then, let's make sure all his flying is directed at you first, shall we?" Anthony retorted, and opening the door to Jason's study, began to immediately place blame where it was due. "Jason, old man, I tried to calm this great hulking bull down last night, indeed I did, but he was having none of it. Blames me—"

"Great hulking bull?" James interrupted, one golden brow raised sharply.

"—because George ain't talking to him," Anthony continued without pause. "And now he's got me in the same bloody boat, because Roslynn ain't said a word to me since."

"Great *hulking* bull?" James repeated.

Anthony glanced at him and smirked, "The shoe fits, believe me."

Jason, standing stiffly behind his desk, snapped at them both, "Enough! I'll hear the whys and wherefores now, if you please."

James smiled. "Yes, you did leave out the best part, Tony."

Anthony sighed and told his elder brother, "It was the worse bloody luck, Jason, indeed it was, and could have happened to any one of us, if truth be told. Jack and Judy managed to sneak into Knighton's Hall while I wasn't looking, and just because I had the care of them that day, I am being blamed because the little darlings came away with a phrase or two that don't belong in their young vocabularies."

"That's dressing it up a bit too nicely," James interjected. "Let's not forget to mention that George didn't blame you a'tall, that she instead blames me, as if I could possibly have known you could be so witless as to take the girls anywhere near—"

"I'll fix things up with George soon as she gets here," Anthony mumbled. "You may depend upon it."

"Oh, I know you will, but you'll have to hie yourself back to London to do so, since she ain't coming here. Didn't want to inflict her dour mood on the festivities, so decided it would be best to absent herself."

Anthony looked appalled now and complained, "You didn't say she was *that* mad."

"Didn't I? Think you're wearing that black eye just because she's a mite annoyed?"

"That will do," Jason said sternly. "This entire situation is intolerable. And frankly, I find it beyond amazing that you have both utterly lost your finesse in dealing with women since you married."

That, of course, hit quite below the belt where these two ex-rakes were concerned. "Ouch," James muttered, then in his own defense, "American women are an exception to any known rule, and bloody stubborn besides."

"So are Scots, for that matter," Anthony added. "They just don't behave like normal Englishwomen, Jason, indeed they don't."

"Regardless. You know my feelings on the *entire* family gathering here for Christmas. This is not the time for *any*one in the family to be harboring *any* ill will of *any* sort. You both should have patched this up before the holidays began. See that you do so immediately, if you both have to return to London to do so."

Having said his peace, Jason headed for the door to leave his brothers to mull over their conduct, or rather, misconduct, but added before he left, "You both look like bloody panda bears. D'you have any idea what kind of example that sets for the children?"

"Panda bears indeed," Anthony snorted as soon as the door closed.

James looked up to reply drolly, "Least the roof is still intact."

Chapter Seven

Though she had said she wasn't coming, James's wife showed up with their children late the next morning. Georgina also had the rest of her brothers in tow, much to James's chagrin, since he never did get along well with his many American brothers-in-law, and he hadn't been warned they were coming to England for Christmas this year.

Judy, delighted that her best friend was finally there, still said huffily, "It's about time," and grabbing Jack the moment she stepped in the front door, pulled her into the parlor to see "The Present," as it was already being termed by then. And the two young girls spent most of the rest of the day with their fingers pressed to the pedestal table, which was nearly as tall as they were, and doing a lot of whispering back and forth about the mysterious gift.

Their avid interest, though, managed to bring The Present back fully to the attention of the adults in the house, who couldn't help noticing the girls more or less standing guard over it. A strange thing, curiosity. Occasionally, too much of it simply couldn't be contained . . .

But in the hall, without much more than a curt nod to Georgina's brothers, though the rest of his family converged on them with greetings, James followed his wife upstairs to the room they always shared at Haverston, while the children's nanny took the twins off to the nursery. She hadn't said a word to him yet, which didn't give him much hope that she was no longer annoyed with him, despite her showing up.

So he reminded her pointedly, "You said you weren't coming, George. What changed your mind?"

She didn't answer immediately, since a footman followed them into the room with one of her trunks, which she moved to start unpacking. James, hearing another one coming down the hall, promptly closed the door and leaned back against it, figuring the servant would get the message that his delivery could wait.

He watched her closely as he waited, no hard chore that. She was quite a beautiful woman, with rich brown hair and eyes of the same hue. She was petite yet nicely rounded; bearing one daughter and a set of twins had only enhanced her figure.

Theirs had been an unusual beginning, hardly what one would call a courtship. Georgina, wanting to return home to America, had signed onto James's ship as his cabin boy. He'd known, of course, that she wasn't the young lad she was pretending to be, and he'd had a splendid, if sometimes frustrated, time seducing her. He hadn't expected to fall in love, though, but that had happened easy enough, to his own jaded amazement. He had, however, sworn never to marry, so it had been a bit of a dilemma, figuring out how to make Georgina his permanently, without actually asking her to marry him.

Her brothers had solved that problem for him nicely. With a little subtle provoking on his part, they had forced him to the altar, which he'd always be grateful to them for, though he'd be twice damned if he'd ever admit that to *them.*

After wrapping up a few loose ends, like getting her to admit she loved him, too, they'd had a wonderful marriage ever since. She might blow up every once in a while— with her hot American temper, she'd never had any trouble expressing her displeasure. But then he'd never had any trouble charming her out of any snit she got into.

Which was why he didn't understand their current spat and why it was continuing as long as it was. When he'd left for Haverston, she still hadn't been speaking to him, hadn't been sleeping with him either, for that matter. And all because their daughter had uttered a few colorful phrases more suited to the adult male gender?

That had been her excuse, but he'd had time and enough to wonder if that was really what had made her temper blow up. It wasn't like Georgina to go overboard on trifles. And to blame him for Jacqueline's vocabulary when he wasn't even responsible for it . . .

"Well?" he prompted when she still hadn't answered.

If somewhat stiffly, she replied, "Thomas convinced me that I might have overreacted about Jack."

James sighed in relief. "Only level-headed brother you've got. I'll remember to thank him later."

"Don't bother. I'm still upset, and you're the reason I'm upset, and I would *really* rather not discuss this just yet, James. I'm here for the children's sake, since Jack has been doing nothing but moping about, knowing that Judy is here while she isn't."

"Bloody hell, then I'm not forgiven yet?"

Her answer was to turn away and continue her unpacking. And he knew that mulish look of hers. She really wasn't going to discuss this with him, whatever it was that she was upset about. He was sure now that it had nothing to do with their daughter. But he was damned if he knew what it could be that she was obviously blaming him for, when he hadn't *done* anything to be blamed for.

And then he noticed her shoulders drooping, a clear indication, to his mind,

that she didn't like this estrangement between them any more than he did. And of
course, she wouldn't. He *knew* she loved
him.

He took a step toward her, but made
the mistake of whispering her name as well.
"George."

She stiffened again, her moment of de-
spair gone and her stubborn streak firmly
back in place. James promptly swore a
blue streak, which fortunately there were no
children about to hear, but unfortunately
had no effect whatsoever in getting Georgina to talk to him again.

Chapter Eight

Later in the afternoon, Edward, the second oldest of the four Malory brothers, arrived with the rest of his family. It was when Edward was being "filled in" by Reggie about what they had discovered concerning the mysterious grave on the property that Amy got the feeling that The Present was not just a present. She felt that it was much more important than a mere gift, that it was actually somehow related to the mystery that was Anna Malory.

And the feeling wouldn't go away once it took root. It was so strong that she made the decision to open the gift that very night. She just was undecided about waiting until Warren fell asleep, or confiding in him. The fact that he didn't seem to be the least bit tired, even after some vigorous lovemaking, settled the matter.

Still held in his arms, with his hands idly caressing her, she whispered by his ear, "I'm going to go downstairs and open The Present tonight."

"Of course you aren't," he replied mildly. "You'll enjoy the suspense and wait until Christmas like the rest of us to find out what it is."

"I wish I could, Warren, really I do, but I know it will drive me crazy, especially after I made a bet with Jeremy, that we would find out about our great-grandmother before the end of the year."

"After Jason expressly forbade it?"

"He didn't exactly forbid it, and besides, it's too late to take it back."

He sat up to look down at her. "And what has that to do with that present?"

"That's just it. I have the strangest feeling that what's in that box is the answer. My feelings are rarely wrong, Warren. And knowing that, how can I wait until Christmas to find out what's in that box?"

He shook his head at her and said in such a disapproving tone that she was reminded of the old Warren who never laughed or smiled, "I would expect such behavior from the children, not from their mother."

She *tsk*ed at him, not even a little daunted. "Aren't you the least bit curious?"

"Certainly, but I can wait until—"

"But I *can't* wait," she cut in passionately. "Come with me, Warren. I'll be careful with it. And if it's nothing more'n a simple gift, albeit a mysterious one, then I'll have the box wrapped up again perfectly, so no one will know we tampered with it."

"You're serious about this?" he asked. "You're actually going to sneak downstairs in the middle of the night like an errant schoolgirl—"

"No, no, *we* are, like two perfectly sensible adults making a reasonable effort to solve a mystery that has been around far too long."

He chuckled at that point, used to his wife's strange logic, *and* used to her ignoring any of his attempts at sternness. But then that was the magic of Amy. She was unlike any other woman he'd ever known.

He gave in gracefully with a smile. "Very

well, fetch our robes *and* some shoes. I would imagine the fire has been banked in the parlor, so it will be a mite chilly."

It wasn't long before they were standing next to The Present, Warren merely curious, Amy finding it hard to contain her excitement, considering what she expected to find beneath the pretty cloth wrapping. The parlor wasn't chilly at all, since whoever had left the room last had closed the doors to contain the earlier warmth, and Warren had closed them again before he lit several of the lamps.

But the doors opened once more, giving Amy quite a start since she was just reaching for The Present when it happened, and Jeremy said as he entered the room, "Caught in the act, eh? Amy, for shame."

Amy, noticeably embarrassed despite the fact that Jeremy wasn't just her cousin, but one of her closest friends, said stiffly, "And what, pray tell, are *you* doing down here at this hour?"

He winked at her and said dryly, "Same thing you are, I would imagine."

She chuckled then. "Scamp. Close the door while you're at it."

He started to, but stepped out of the way instead as Reggie sauntered in, barefoot and still in the process of tying her bed robe. When everyone else there just stared at her, she huffed indignantly, "I did *not* come down here to open The Present— well, maybe I did, but I *would* have chickened out before actually doing so."

"What a whopper, Reggie," Derek said as he came in right behind her. "Nice try, though. Mind if I borrow that lame excuse? Better than having none a'tall."

And Kelsey, close on his heels, said, "You amaze me, Derek. You said we'd be lucky if we were the first to open it, and goodness, you couldn't have been more right."

"Not a'tall, m'dear." He grinned at his wife. "Just know my cousins very well."

He did indeed, because next to arrive were Amy's brothers, Travis and Marshall, shoving their way through the doorway, or trying to, at the same time. So it took a moment for them to realize they weren't alone.

But one look at the crowd already present had Travis grumbling to his older brother, "Told you this wasn't a good idea."

"On the contrary, looks like we ain't the only ones who had it," Marshall replied cheerfully.

"Hell's bells, does the whole family think alike?" Jeremy asked with a chuckle.

"Hardly," Amy answered. "You don't see Uncle Jason and my father here, do you? Nor Uncle James and Tony. Not that those latter two don't think alike, they just don't think like the rest of us."

But there was a cough out in the hall that had Amy rolling her eyes, then grinning when she heard Anthony say, "Now, why do I get the feeling the younguns think we're too old to be up this time of night?"

"Harping about our ages *again,* dear boy?" James shot back. "You might be getting senile, but I'll have you know I'm in my prime."

"Deuced hard for me to get senile before you, old man, since you're the elder," Anthony pointed out with a good deal of pleasure.

"By one bloody year," James was heard to reply before they walked into the parlor.

Unlike their nieces and nephews, who were all in their bedclothes, James and Anthony were both still fully clothed, since neither had gone to bed yet. They had in fact been commiserating over a bottle of brandy in Jason's study, since they'd both found their bedroom doors locked to them, and had heard one too many creaks on the stairs not to investigate.

They hadn't expected to find quite such a large gathering, however, and Anthony couldn't resist remarking, "My, my, now, what would draw so many children to this room in the middle of the night, I wonder? Jack and Judy aren't hiding behind you, are they? D'you get the feeling these younguns think it's Christmas already, James?"

James had already deduced what was causing so many red faces, and said, "Good God, take a gander at that, Tony. Even the Yank is blushing, damn me if he ain't."

Warren sighed and glanced down at his wife. "You see what your silliness has caused, love? Those two will never let me live this down."

"Course we will," Anthony replied with

a wicked grin. "In ten or twenty years per-haps."

"If I'm right about what's in The Present, then no one will be calling this silliness," Amy said.

"*What's* in it?" Marshall piped up, star-ing at his sister. "You mean you've guessed what it is? You're not just here out of cu-riosity?"

"I made the bet with Jeremy," Amy ex-plained, as if that was explanation enough.

It was actually, but Reggie reminded her, "Even after Uncle Jason pretty much forbade it?"

Jeremy blinked. "Hell's bells, cousin, you didn't tell me I wasn't *supposed* to ac-cept your wager."

"Well, of course not, then you wouldn't have," Amy replied in perfect logic.

And Warren added, "Don't even try to figure that out, Jeremy. When she gets one of her 'feelings,' she gives new meaning to the word 'determination.' "

"Would have said 'mulish' myself, but I suppose you know her better than I these days."

"Oh, bosh," Amy mumbled, giving them

a disgusted look. "You both will have my permission to eat your words, since I *am* going to be proven right."

Reggie said, "You actually think The Present has something to do with our great-grandmother?"

"I do," Amy replied excitedly. "When I first saw it, I had the feeling that it was important. But today I got the feeling that it was now related to my bet, so it *must* have something to do with Anna Malory."

"Let's not talk it into the ground, children, or we'll be here all night," James said. "Just open the bloody thing and be done with it."

Amy grinned at her uncle and did just that. But no one was expecting that under the wrapping, The Present would still be difficult to get at—under padlock to be exact.

Chapter Nine

The silence that settled on the room as everyone stared bemusedly at the padlock on top of The Present was finally broken by one of James's drier tones as he said, "I take it no one has the key?"

Whatever the gift was, it was bound tightly in thick leather that had been cut to fold over it in triangular flaps, each flap having a metal ring on the end of it that allowed the padlock to lock them all together. It was very old-looking leather. The padlock was also rusty, indicating it was very old as well, so obviously, whatever was under it would be just as old.

That, of course, lent credence to Amy's feeling that The Present might be relevant to Anna Malory in some way. Yet no one could yet guess how, or what it was, and especially who had put it there. The shape of it could be a book, but why would someone lock up a book? It was more likely a book-shaped box with something smaller in it, something of great value, something, as far as Amy was concerned, that would point clearly to Anna Malory's true ancestry. She tried to lift one of the flaps a bit to see if she could see under it, but the leather was just too stiff and tightly drawn to budge.

"An attached key would have been too simple, I suppose." Reggie sighed.

"The leather was cut to shape around it. It can be cut to unwrap it," Derek pointed out.

"So it can," James agreed, and reached down to lift a very sharp-looking dagger out of his boot. That, of course, had Anthony raising a brow at him, to which he replied with a shrug, "Old habits are hard to break."

"Quite so, and you did haunt some of the more disreputable waterfront establishments in your day, didn't you?" Anthony remarked.

"Are we doing the laundry now, or getting inside that box?" James shot back.

Anthony chuckled. "The box, of course, old man. Do slice away."

The leather was tougher to cut than they imagined it would be, particularly with so little room for a blade to slip under any of the flaps to do the job. In the end, it was more James's strength than the dagger that snapped the leather away from the rings, so the padlock could be set aside and the flaps peeled back.

He handed it back to Amy to do the honors. She wasted not a moment pulling the flaps out of the way and lifting the gift out. It was a book after all, leather-bound and untitled. There was also a folded parchment in it that fell out and floated to the floor.

Though a half dozen hands reached for it, Derek picked it up first, unfolded it, and after a quick glance, said, "Good God, Amy, you really do know how to call 'em, don't you? I hope you didn't wager too much, Jeremy."

Jeremy chuckled at that. "She wasn't interested in winning anything, just in making the bet so she *would* win it. Works for her every bloody time, if you ain't noticed.

Ought to drag her to the races one of these days. She'd even put old Percy to shame in picking winners, and he's been amazingly lucky himself in that regard."

Percy was an old friend of the family, at least of the younger generation. He'd chummed about with Nicholas, Derek, and then Jeremy as well, when Derek took his newly found cousin under his wing years ago.

"If you don't say what's in that letter this instant, Derek Malory, I'm going to kick you, see if I don't," Reggie said impatiently.

She and Derek were more like brother and sister than cousins, having been raised together after Reggie's mother died, and she had been known to kick him quite frequently over the years, so he was quick to reply, "It's a journal they wrote together, a history so to speak. Gads, that was nice of them, considering there's no one left alive who knew them—*really* knew them, that is."

He handed the parchment to Reggie, who shared it aloud with the others.

To our children and their children and so forth,

This record we leave to you may be a surprise, or it may not. It's not something we talk of other than in private, nor have we ever told our son. And we are not assured of having more children that we may or may not speak of it to.

Know that it was not an easy task, getting my husband to agree to add his thoughts to this record, because he feels he does not express himself well with the written word. In the end, I had to promise him that I would not read his portion, so he would be free to include feelings and perspectives that I might not agree with, or might tease him about. He made me the same promise; thus, when we finished this record, we did securely lock it and throw away the key.

So we leave this written record to you, to be read at your leisure, and with your own imagination lend-

ing it life. Though when you do read it, it will most likely be when we are no longer with you to be questioned about our motives and less than honest dealings with the people who would do us harm. And I give you fair warning: If you have been led to believe that we are individuals that could do no wrong, then read no further. We are human, after all, with all the faults, passions, and mistakes that humans are known for. Judge us not, but perhaps learn from our mistakes.

Anastasia Malory

Amy was beaming widely as she held the journal to her chest. She'd been right! And she wanted to start reading this unexpected gift from her great-grandparents immediately, but the others were still discussing the letter . . .

"Anastasia?" Anthony was saying. "Can't say I've ever heard my grandmother called that before."

"It's not exactly an English name, is it, whereas Anna is," James pointed out. "An obvious effort to conceal the truth, if you ask me."

"But what truth?" Derek asked. "Anastasia could be a Spanish name."

"Or not," Travis put in.

Marshall said, "No need to speculate at this point, when we'll be reading the truth for ourselves. So who gets to read it first?"

"Amy does, of course," Derek suggested. "It might have shown up before she made that bet with Jeremy, but it's related as far as I'm concerned, though I'd still like to know who found it and wrapped it up for a Christmas gift, rather than just give it to m'father."

"It's likely been in this house all these years, with no one aware of it," Reggie speculated.

"I'll buy that," Derek said. "Hell, this house is so big, there's places in it even I haven't looked into, and I was raised here."

"Lot of us were born and raised here, dear boy," Anthony mentioned. "But you're right, not every little thing gets investigated when you're young. Depends what you find interesting, I suppose."

Amy couldn't stand the suspense anymore and offered at that point, "I'm willing to read it aloud, if some of you want to stay to hear it."

"I'm game for a chapter or two at least," Marshall said, and found himself a seat to get comfortable in.

"As thick as that journal is, it may take right up to Christmas day to get it all read," Warren noted as he sat on one of the couches and patted the spot next to him for Amy to settle into.

"Lucky then we opened it ahead of time, eh?" Jeremy grinned.

"Can't very well get to sleep now, not after that 'Judge us not, but perhaps learn from our mistakes,' " James said. "Too bloody intriguing, that."

"Think we should wake the elders first, though," Anthony replied.

James nodded. "I agree. You wake them while I find us another bottle of brandy. I get the feeling it's going to be a long bloody night."

Chapter Ten

There were four large wagons in the caravan. Three of them were nearly little houses on wheels, made entirely of wood, including the slightly curved roof, and replete with a door and windows covered in bright curtains. Some were ancient, a testimony to the superior quality of craftsmanship that made them. Even the fourth wagon showed this quality, though it was merely a typical supply wagon.

When the caravan would move off to the side of a road at night to make camp, tents would be removed from the fourth wagon, along with large kettles and the iron rods that formed triangles over campfires to hold them, and the food to throw into them. Within minutes of the caravan halting, the area would take on the atmosphere of a small, cheerful village. Pleasant aromas would drift off into the surrounding woods, as well as the gay sound of music and laughter.

The largest of the four wagons belonged to the *barossan,* the leader, Ivan Lautaru. Surrounding his wagon were the tents of his family, his wife's sisters, her mother, his sisters, and his unmarried daughters.

The second largest wagon belonged to Ivan's son, Nicolai, built in preparation for him to take a wife. It had been built six years ago. He had yet to take that wife. The omens were not right for it, according to Maria Stephanoff, the old woman who lived in the third wagon. First she claimed the wedding must take place on a certain day of the year to be fruitful, then she claimed each year that the omens weren't right for it on the appointed day, much to Nicolai's fury.

There were a total of six families in the small caravan, with forty-six people among them, including the children. They intermarried as they were able, yet sometimes there were not enough brides or grooms to choose from, from so few families, and in such times they would search for other caravans like theirs in hopes there would be marriageable young ones in the same need. They met and dealt with countless people in their travels, yet these were outsiders, *Gajos,* and those of pure blood would never consider these outsiders for marriage.

Ivan was losing patience with the delay of his son's wedding as well. He had already paid the bride price for this wife for Nicolai. His word was law, yet he would not gainsay Maria. She was their luck, their good fortune. To ignore Maria's predictions would be the death of them. They firmly believed this. Yet he could not choose another bride for his son either. Only Maria's granddaughter would do, her only living descendant, the only one who could continue to bring them their good fortune when Maria passed on.

Tonight, as usual, they made camp near the town they had passed through during the day. They never camped too close to a town, just close enough to give the townsfolk easy access to them, and vice versa. In the morning the women would walk to the town and knock on every door, offering their services, be it the selling of trinkets or finely made baskets, or the telling of fortunes, which their caravan was known for.

They would also advertise the skills of their men, for the Lautaru caravan possessed some of the finest wagonmakers in the world. Everything earned was shared by all, for ownership of property was alien to them. Which was why a few of those women might come home with a stolen chicken or two.

If a wagon was ordered, they might stay in the vicinity for a week; if not, they would be gone within a day or two. Occasionally, if it was taking too long, they would leave the wagonmakers behind to catch up with them once their job was finished. Signs would be left along the roads to guide them back to the caravan.

This was necessary when people such as they were the scapegoats for any crime, whether they committed it or not. If caravans like theirs were in the area, fingers would begin to point at them if they were there too long. They could make camp within minutes; they could pack up and leave even quicker. From long experience and the persecution of their kind for centuries, they had learned to be able to be back on the road again on a moment's notice.

They were wanderers; it was in their blood, the need to travel, to see what was over the next horizon. The young adults had seen most of Europe. The older ones had seen Russia, and the countries surrounding it. They tended to stay in a country long enough to learn its language fairly well, if circumstances didn't chase them out beforehand. A wealth of languages was a benefit to any traveler. Ivan prided himself on knowing sixteen different languages.

This was not their first visit to England, nor would it likely be their last, since the English laws dealing with them were not as harsh as they had been in centuries past. They found the English a strange people actually. Many young Englishmen of good family were so fascinated by their beliefs and love of freedom that they wanted to join them, to dress like them, to act like them.

Ivan would tolerate one or two of these *Gajos* for short periods of time, only because their presence had a calming effect on the English peasants, who would reason that if their own English lords found these people to be trustworthy, then they couldn't be the thieves they were reputed to be, now could they?

There was one such *Gajo* with them now, Sir William Thompson. He was not the usual sort to want to join them, far from it. He was an old man, older even than Maria, and she was the oldest among them. She had deigned to speak to him several months ago, not to tell his fortune, which she no longer did for *Gajos,* but because she had seen the pain in his eyes and had wanted to remove it.

This she did, relieving William of a guilt he had been burdened with for over forty years, so that he could go to his Maker in peace. He was so grateful, he swore to devote his remaining years to Maria. In truth, he had realized that she was dying, and wanted to make her last days as pleasant as he could, in repayment for what she had done for him. No one else knew. Those who had known Maria all their lives didn't know. Her own granddaughter didn't know. Yet William had guessed, and it was an unspoken knowledge between them.

Ivan, though, would not have permitted him to stay. His age was a detriment, it was decided. He was too old to contribute to the community coffers. But he demanded to prove himself and did, always returning to the camp with his pockets full of coins, so he was allowed to stay. It was a moot point, really, that he was a wealthy man and the coins were his own. He was merely paying for the privilege to remain near Maria. Besides, he ended up making a further contribution, in bettering their English, which was a good thing, since they had no plans to leave England this year.

Anastasia Stephanoff sat on the stoop of the wagon she shared with Maria, her grandmother next to her. They watched the camp as it settled down for the night. The campfires were banked. A few groups still sat around them talking quietly. Children were rolled up in their blankets wherever they had gotten drowsy. Sir William, whom they had more or less adopted, was snoring loudly under their own wagon.

Anastasia had become very fond of Sir William in the short time they had known him. She found him silly most of the time, in his courtly ways, his stiff hauteur that was so English, in his efforts to make Maria laugh. But there was nothing silly in his devotion to her grandmother, a devotion that was not in doubt.

She would often tease Maria that it was too bad she was too old for romance, to which she would usually get a chuckle, a wink, and the remark "There is never an age too old for romance. Lovemaking, now, that is a different matter. Some bones get too brittle for such nice exercise as that."

Romance, lovemaking, these were not subjects that might only be spoken of in embarrassed whispers. Their people would discuss anything openly and with passion that they found to be natural, and what could be more natural than romance and lovemaking?

Lovemaking was brought clearly to mind as Anastasia watched her future husband push his current lover toward his wagon. He was not gentle about it. The woman even stumbled and fell. He yanked her back to her feet by her hair and pushed her again. Anastasia shuddered. Nicolai was a vicious brute. She had felt the sting of his palm many times herself, when he did not like the way she talked back to him. And this was the man she was to marry.

Maria noticed the shudder, and the direction of her gaze. "It bothers you, that he makes love to others?"

"I wish it did, Gran, then I would not feel so hopeless about my future. Any woman is welcome to him as far as I am concerned, though I cannot understand how they can abide him, as mean as he is."

Maria shrugged. "The prestige, of being favored by Ivan's only son."

Anastasia snorted indelicately. "There is nothing but pain in such favor. I hear he is not even a good lover, that he takes his pleasure and gives none in return."

"There are many selfish men like that. His father was the same."

Anastasia grinned. "You know that from personal experience, Gran?"

"Pshaw, Ivan should have been so lucky. No, the *barossan* and I always had a perfect understanding of each other. He would not look at me with lust in his eyes, and I would not curse him to the end of his days."

Anastasia laughed. "Yes, that might tend to make a man a bit leery of you."

Maria smiled, but then her expression became serious, and she reached over to fold her gnarled fingers with Anastasia's. The young woman felt alarm rising. Maria did not hold her hand unless there was bad news to impart. She could not imagine what that bad news could be, but she held her breath with dread, for Maria's bad news tended to be really, really bad news of the devastating sort.

Chapter Eleven

Anastasia had turned eighteen a few months ago. That was considered far, far beyond the marriageable age, when twelve was considered just right among their people.

Some of the women teased her mercilessly, for not knowing the touch of a man yet. Foolish, to waste her best years. Foolish to not gain extra coins from the *Gajos* for a quick tumble. It was just another way to fleece them. It meant nothing. No husband, or future husband, would be jealous of it; they in fact *expected* it. Only if a husband caught his wife making eyes at another member of the band would there be serious consequences; divorce, severe beatings, sometimes death, or worse in their eyes, banishment.

Whenever Anastasia would talk to Maria about her feelings on this matter, that she felt such an aversion to the very thought of being touched by man after man after man, Maria would blame it on her father's blood. Many things over the years had been attributed to her father, some bad, some good. Maria had found him to be a wonderful scapegoat, when she could think of no other way to answer Anastasia's questions.

Many things flitted through Anastasia's mind as she waited for Maria's bad news, things other than speculation of what that news would be. She could guess if she put her mind to it, but she didn't want to know, not yet. The continued silence was a balm at first; it did not contain disaster. But it lasted too long. Suspense intruded, and became unbearable.

Finally Anastasia could stand it no longer and prompted, "What is it, Gran, that you do not want to tell me?"

A sigh, a brief, heartfelt one. "Something that I have delayed far too long, child. Two things, actually, both of which will cause you considerable distress. The distress, you are strong enough to deal with. The abrupt change that will occur to your life is what worries me, and why I want to see it done soonest, while I am here to aid you."

"You have foreseen something?"

Maria shook her head sadly. "I only wish I did know the future in this instance. But you must make that future yourself, and the decision you make will be for your good or ill, but it must be made. The alternative, you have said yourself, is unthinkable."

Anastasia knew then, what Maria was being so cryptic about. Her marriage, or rather, the husband she was to marry. "This is about Nicolai?"

"It is about marriage, yes. I must see you settled into it this week. It can wait no longer."

Anastasia panicked. "But the day you set, it is not for another two months!"

"This cannot wait until then."

"But you know I hate him, Gran!"

"Yes, and if only *you* had known it before I accepted the bride-price for you, then you could have married another long ago. But Ivan, that wily son of a goat, he came to me when you were only seven, five years before you would be old enough to marry, long before you realized that Nicolai would not suit you. Ivan, he was taking no chances, that someone else would beat him to you."

"I was so young," Anastasia said bitterly. "I cannot understand such haste. He could have waited until I was old enough to decide the matter for myself."

"Ah, but we were visiting with another band, you see. And the other *barossan* showed too much interest in our family, and asked too many questions about you. Ivan was no fool. He asked for you that night. The other *barossan* asked for you the next morning, a few hours too late. Ivan gloated over that for many years."

"Yes, I've heard him do so."

"Well, it is time for his gloating to end. He has always used underhanded means to keep me and mine bound to this band because of our gift of insight. I never told you, but when your mother announced that she was going to live with her *Gajo,* Ivan came to me and promised he would kill her before he let her waste her talent on those not of the blood—unless I agreed to bear another child to replace her. I was past childbearing years at the time, but did that fool take that into account?" Maria snorted.

"I take it you must have agreed?"

"Of course." Maria grinned. "I have never had any difficulty lying to Ivan Lautaru."

"Did he badger you about it?"

"No, there was no need. We learned soon enough that your mother was pregnant with you, and Ivan convinced himself that she would return to us with her child, which is why we did not leave that area. It is the longest ever that we have remained in one place."

"But why do you want me to marry Nicolai now? You have helped me to avoid it all these years. What has changed your mind?"

"My mind is not changed, Anna. I said nothing about marrying Nicolai, just that you must marry."

Anastasia's eyes widened, for this had never occurred to her. "Marry someone else? But how can I, when I have been bought and paid for?"

"Marry someone else among us? No, you cannot. It would be the gravest insult to Ivan. Nicolai would never accept such an insult either. He would kill whoever you would choose. But a *Gajo* would be another matter."

"A *Gajo*?" Anastasia said incredulously. "An outsider not of the blood? How can you even suggest it?"

"How can I not, child, when it is your only alternative—unless you wish to live under Nicolai's fist the rest of your life?"

As earlier, Anastasia shuddered. She had long known that she would leave the band first, before she would submit to Nicolai. And what difference, leaving or marrying an outsider? Either way, she would be leaving.

She sighed. "I suppose you have a plan, Gran? Please tell me that you do."

The old woman patted her hand with a smile. "Of course I do, and a very simple one at that. You must bewitch a *Gajo* into asking to marry you. Then you must convince the band that you love him. Love makes the difference on how this will be viewed. One can betray one's people and

all that one believes in, for love. This is un-
derstandable, acceptable. You must be
convincing, though. If it is thought that you
do this just to avoid marrying Nicolai, then
the Lautarus are insulted. You will do as
your mother did. For her it was real. She
really did love her *Gajo.* For you it will be
a lie, but one used to escape the future
you say you cannot accept. And perhaps,
if you are lucky, it will not remain a lie."

Do as her mother had done? Maria's
daughter, Anastasia's mother, had fallen in
love with a Russian boyar, one of the
princeling nobles in that land. She had died
giving birth to his child, a child he would
have kept if it had been a son. But he had
no use for a daughter, and so Maria had
been allowed to take her granddaughter
and raise her.

Anastasia had never met her father, nor
had she ever had the desire to. She didn't
even know if he still lived. She didn't care.
A man who had found no value in her was
nothing to her. And if she carried a small
bit of bitterness in her heart over his rejec-
tion of her, she kept it to herself.

Maria knew how she felt, of course. Maria knew everything. She could look into people's eyes and know exactly what was in their heart. Nothing could be hidden from Maria. But Maria did not always have the answers to the questions that went against the natural philosophies of their people, which was when she would conveniently use the Russian as an excuse.

She did this now, reminding Anastasia, "You are different from the rest of us. Your father's blood shows in this. But that is not a bad thing. You have never stolen, never told a *Gajo* a lie to fleece him of a few coins. These are natural things for us to do, and to brag of, making fools of *Gajos,* yet you scorn such behavior. In that you are your father's daughter, too noble of blood to belittle yourself in what you would deem dishonorable ways. I never tried to break this in you or teach you any differently. It is a good thing to have qualities from both parents, if both parents had good qualities for you to inherit."

"I never wanted to be different."

"I know," Maria said softly. "But one cannot help what one is born to be."

"But won't Ivan threaten to kill me if I leave, as he did my mother?"

"No, not this time. I will convince him that if he keeps you from your love, your broken heart will more likely bring him disaster, rather than good fortune. I will also remind him that you could divorce your *Gajo* at any time and return to the band. This is something you *can* do, Anna, so keep that in mind if you find yourself unhappy in your choice. And if you do return, you will not have to worry about Nicolai ever again. Your marriage to a *Gajo* will break your contract with the Lautarus. You can then do as you please, marry whom you please, marry no one if you please. The choice will once again be yours to be made at your leisure."

"But I know nothing of bewitching men. How can I do this? You expect too much of me."

"Do not doubt yourself, child. Look at you. This band has never seen a prettier woman. You have your mother's glorious black hair with just enough curl to look wanton. You have your father's purest blue eyes, his fair skin. You have your mother's insight, her compassion. Many was the fight she got into with the band, to protect some *Gajo* she felt sorry for. You have done the same. You bewitch every man who looks at you. You just do not notice, because until now, you have not cared."

"I just do not see how this can be done, in so short a time. Two months—"

"One week," Maria cut in adamantly.

"But—"

"One week, Anna, no longer. Go to that town near here tomorrow. Look carefully at every man you see. Speak to those who interest you. Use your talent to help you. But make a choice, then bring him to me. I will know if he is a good choice."

"But do I want a good choice?"

A question like that might have caused confusion in another, but not Maria. "You think to just use this man for a short time, then divorce him so you can return to the band? Only you can answer, child, if you can live with using a man this way. I would have no difficulty doing so, but I am not you. I think you would prefer to be happy in your choice, to make your first marriage be your only marriage."

Maria was right, of course. Going from marriage to marriage was not much different than going from man to man. Anastasia, at least, didn't see much difference in the two. She saw love as lasting forever. Anything less could not really be love.

Unfortunately, she didn't see how, under the time constraint Maria was giving her, she could possibly find a man, an Englishman at that, whom she would want to *stay* married to. She was about to question the time constraint again when Maria's expression, for the second time, turned very serious, and her hand was once again gripped by those gnarled fingers.

"There is something else that I must tell you, that I have also delayed too long in the telling. I will not be leaving this place."

Anastasia frowned, thinking Maria meant to stay here with her and the English husband she was to find. But as much as she would love that to be possible, she knew Ivan would never permit it.

Hating to do so, she had to point that out. "You have told me countless times that Ivan will not let you leave, that he would kill you first."

Maria smiled ironically. "There is nothing he can do to prevent my leaving this time, Anna. The privilege of age will not be denied a final resting place, and I have chosen this place. My time has come."

"No!"

"Shush, daughter of my heart. This is not something that can be debated or bargained aside. And I have no desire to prolong the inevitable. I welcome this gladly, to end the pains that have burdened my body these last few years. I just must see you settled first, or I will not go in peace . . . Now, stop that. There is no need for tears, for something that is so natural as the death of a very old woman."

Anastasia threw her arms around her grandmother, hiding her face against her shoulder so she would no longer see the tears that were absolutely impossible to stop. Maria had predicted distress. Distress was not exactly what Anastasia was feeling just now, with her world falling apart around her. This was much too much to withstand all at once.

But for Maria's sake, she said, "I will do

whatever is necessary to give you your peace."

"I knew you would, child," Maria said, patting her back soothingly. "And you see now why you must be married first? If you are all that Ivan has left, then he won't let you go no matter the reasoning. As long as he *thinks* he still has me, then he will let you go. Now take yourself to bed. You need a good night's sleep so you will have all your wits about you tomorrow, for tomorrow you search for your fate."

Chapter Twelve

"And whose bed was she found in this week?"

"Lord Maldon's. Really thought he had more sense. He must realize she's got the pox by now, in her vain attempt to outdo the last great court Delilah."

"And what makes you think he don't already have it himself?"

"Hmmm, yes, I suppose it wouldn't matter then, would it? Ah, well, there's not much to be said for variety these days. Stick with a mistress that you keep to yourself, like I do. Might live longer that way."

"Why don't you just get married, then, if you want to stick with just one woman?"

"Gads, no. Nothing will put you in the grave quicker than a nagging wife. Do bite your tongue next time, before you make such an outlandish suggestion. 'Sides, what's marriage got to do with keeping to just one woman?"

Christopher Malory was only vaguely listening to his friends' gossip. He shouldn't have brought them with him. They would expect to be entertained, were already showing signs of boredom as they sprawled in their chairs in his estate office, gossiping about *old* gossip. But he didn't come to Haverston to entertain. He came twice a year to go over the account books, which he was trying to do this evening, then leave as quickly as possible.

It was not that he had any business or social engagements in London to draw him back in haste. It was that he never felt comfortable in Haverston, felt actually oppressed if he stayed too long.

It was a dark, gloomy place, with outdated furnishings, ugly grays and dull tans in the wall coverings throughout, even dour-looking servants who never said a word to him other than "Yes, m'lord," or "No, m'lord." He supposed he could redecorate it, but why bother, when he had no desire to remain in Haverston any longer than it took to go over the books and listen to his estate manager's complaints?

It was a fine enough estate in size and income, but he hadn't wanted or needed it. He'd already possessed a very nice estate in Ryding that he rarely visited either—he just didn't care for the quiet of country living—as well as the title of viscount. But Haverston had been given to him in gratitude, along with a lofty new title, for having unwittingly saved the king's life.

It hadn't been intentional, his helping the king. It had occurred purely by accident when he'd stepped out of his mired coach into the road at just the moment that a runaway horse was tearing past. He happened to startle the horse into stopping, whereupon the horse had dumped its rider more or less into Christopher's lap, as it were; at least Christopher had ended up flattened on the ground with a hefty weight on top of him.

As queer circumstances would have it, the rider turned out to be his king, who had been hunting in the nearby woods when his horse had been spooked by a small animal. King George, of course, had been exceedingly grateful for the interference which he swore had saved his life. And there'd been no talking him out of being quite generous in his gratitude.

His manager, Artemus Whipple, was sitting across the desk from him and avidly listening to the gossip, rather than the business at hand. Christopher had to say his name twice to draw his attention back to his last question, and repeat it once again.

Whipple was a portly, middle-aged man who had come with the estate, and Christopher had found no reason, really, to replace him. As long as the estate produced an income, which it did, he could hardly fault him, even if some of the expenses he incurred could boggle the mind. He *did* always have a ready excuse for them. But some were so outlandish, they demanded questioning.

"Fifty pounds for laborers to plow and plant the home farm? Did you ship them in from the Americas?"

Whipple noted the sarcasm and blushed uncomfortably. "They were outrageously overpriced, yes, but it's getting increasingly more difficult to find farmers to work here. There's a silly rumor that Haverston is haunted and that's why you won't stay in residence."

Christopher rolled his eyes. "What rubbish."

"Oh, I say," Walter Keats interjected. "First interesting thing I've heard since we got here. Who's the haunter supposed to be?"

Walter, the youngest of the three friends at twenty-eight, was the one who abhorred the thought of marriage. His powdered wig was askew at the moment, after an itch had been scratched absentmindedly. Though wigs, and powered ones at that, were mostly worn only on formal occasions these days, Walter took his cue from the older aristocracy and didn't leave his dressing room without one. Fact was, it was vanity and nothing more, since his dull brown hair didn't give him quite the flair that a perfectly powered wig did, coupled with his vivid green eyes.

"Who?" Whipple asked the young lord with a blank look, as if he hadn't expected his reason to be dissected, and in fact,

Christopher rarely did question him further on any of his given excuses.

"Yes, who?" Walter persisted, putting the manager on the spot. "If a place is haunted, stands to reason some*one* is doing the haunting, now don't it?"

Whipple's blush increased as he said stiffly, "I really wouldn't know, Lord Keats. I don't give much credence to peasant superstition."

"Nor does it matter," Christopher added. "There are no ghosts here."

Walter sighed. "You're such a stick, Kit. If my home had history, as in the blood and gore type, I'd bloody well want to know it."

"I don't consider this my home, Walter."

"Whyever not?"

Christopher gave a careless shrug. "The town house in London has always been my home. This place is just a place—a chore."

David Rutherford, not as plump in the pockets as his two friends, shook his head. "Who but Kit would consider a place like this just a place. It does look a bit drab, I'll allow, but it's got such potential."

David, at thirty, wasn't quite as bored yet with life as Christopher was at thirty-two. He was handsome by any standards with his black hair and very light blue eyes, and most of his interests these days were centered around women, though he was game to try anything new, and especially anything that sounded the least bit adventurous or dangerous.

Christopher wished he felt the same, but he had developed a strange ennui this last year and couldn't seem to find any interest in *anything.* He had come to realize that he was bored with all aspects of his life. It was a boredom that was beginning to weigh heavily on his mind.

With his parents dying when he was quite young, and having no other relatives, he had been raised by the family solicitor and servants, who perhaps gave him a different outlook on things. He did not find amusing what his friends did. Actually, he found very little about his life amusing anymore, which was why his boredom had become so noticeable.

"Whatever potential Haverston has would depend on time and inclination," Christopher replied tiredly.

"You've got the time," Walter pointed out. "So it must be lack of inclination."

"Exactly," Christopher said with a pointed look that he hoped would end the discussion, but just to be sure, he added, "Now, if you two don't mind, I *do* have work to do here. I'd like to return to London before autumn."

Since that season was a good month away, his sarcasm was duly noted and the two younger gentlemen exchanged aggrieved looks and got back to their gossiping. But Christopher no sooner glanced down at the next entry in the estate books when the butler arrived to announce some unexpected visitors from Havers Town.

The mayor, the Reverend Biggs, and Mr. Stanley, oldest member of Havers's town council, had each shown up to welcome Christopher to the "neighborhood" on his first trip to Haverston several years ago. He had seen none of these men again, however, since there had been no occasion to visit the nearby town when he was in residence, and he couldn't imagine what would bring them to Haverston again, particularly so late of an evening. They didn't leave him guessing, though, got right to the point of their visit.

"We were invaded today, Lord Malory."

"By a bunch of ungodly thieves and sellers of sin," Reverend Biggs said most indignantly.

Walter latched on to the word "ungodly," asking, "These are different from Godly thieves, I take it?"

He was being sarcastic, but the good reverend took him seriously instead, answering stiffly, "Heathens usually are, m'lord."

David, however, had perked up considerably at the mention of sin. "What kind of sin were they selling?"

But Christopher, annoyed at yet another interruption to his chore, wanted to know, "Why do you bring this matter to me? Why didn't you just have these criminals arrested?"

"Because they weren't *caught* stealing. They are very clever, these heathens."

Christopher impatiently waved that aside, since his question still hadn't been answered. "As mayor, you can just ask them to leave your good town, so I repeat, why do you bring this matter to me?"

"Because the Gypsies aren't staying in our town, Lord Malory, they are camping on your property, where we have no jurisdiction."

"Gypsies? Oh, *that* kind of sin," David said with a chuckle that earned him a disapproving frown from the reverend.

"So I take it you want *me* to ask them to leave?" Christopher said.

"Course he does, Kit. And Walter and I will come along to assist you. Couldn't let you go alone, now could we? Never think it."

Christopher rolled his eyes. His friends had found something to entertain themselves, after all, and by the look of them both, were quite looking forward to it.

Chapter Thirteen

"I've never seen so many married men in one place," Anastasia said in complete disgust as she joined her grandmother at their campfire that night. "For such a nice-sized town, it was sadly lacking for our purpose, Gran. I couldn't find a single man who wasn't either too old, too young, or too—unacceptable."

"Not *one?*" Maria said in surprise.

"None."

Maria frowned thoughtfully before asking, "What kind of 'unacceptable'?"

"The kind that it would never be believed that I would fall in love with."

Maria sighed with a nod. "No, that kind won't do. Very well, I will tell Ivan tonight that we must leave. He will not question why. You can try the next town."

"I thought you said you wanted to stay here, that you find this clearing a peaceful place to rest."

"So I will look for a peaceful place down the road. Do not worry about me, child. I have the will to last until you wed—as long as you wed within the week."

Anastasia's shoulders drooped upon hearing that. She had promised herself that she wouldn't cry again. If her grandmother really was suffering in her old age, then she would be truly selfish to wish her to remain with the living just because she knew she was going to be utterly lost without her love and guidance.

So little time left. So much she wanted to say to this woman who had raised her. So many things she wanted to thank her for. But she could think of nothing adequate enough to express it all, except . . .

"I love you, Gran."

Maria's face lit up with a smile and she reached over and squeezed Anastasia's hand. "You will do fine, daughter of my heart. Your instincts will guide you, your insight will aid you; these things I predict for you. But if you or yours ever need my help, you will have it."

It was a fanciful claim, to offer help from the beyond, yet it still gave Anastasia immense comfort. She returned the squeeze and, to take the edge off their seriousness, teased, "You will be too busy, fending off all those handsome angels that have been waiting for you."

"Pshaw! What do I want with more choices to make, when it's peace I'm looking for?"

"Excellent point," Sir William said as he joined them at the fire. "And besides, she will be waiting for me, so there won't be any choices to make between those handsome angels, who, alas, will be infinitely disappointed." He bowed to Maria, then dumped a handful of wildflowers into her lap. "Good evening, m'dear."

Anastasia smiled as she observed Maria's slight blush and the adoring look that the Englishman gave her. Another reason she liked William so much—he was good for her grandmother, was adding pleasure to her last days. She would always be grateful to him for that.

He didn't stay long, though, since the food Maria was cooking wasn't ready yet, and he took it upon himself to tend to her wagon horses several times each day. But no sooner did he move off toward the horses than some unexpected visitors arrived in the camp.

It was quite an entrance, three riders galloping in, stopping abruptly, one of the horses a large brown stallion that looked annoyed to have his brisk ride curtailed, if his tossing head, stomping feet, and, finally, rearing up on his back legs were any indication.

His rider controlled him admirably, though, and got him to settle down after a few moments. Anastasia looked at this man who could so easily handle such a powerful horse, and looked no further, was for the first time actually mesmerized by the sight of someone.

He was big, very big and broad of shoulder, thick of chest. His hair was blond, unpowdered. Half the English people she came across wore wigs, men and women alike, and half of those wore them powdered. But if that thick, tied-back golden mane was a wig, it was superbly made and lacking the tightly rolled curls at the temples that the English found so fashionable.

He was amazingly handsome, at least Anastasia found him to be so, which was why she was so mesmerized, and why Maria, watching her stare at him, said, "So you have found one today after all."

"He could be married," Anastasia said in a small, awed voice.

"No," Maria said adamantly. "It is your time to be lucky, child. Now, go take control of your fate, before one of the other women gains his attention and you must wrest him from her. They would be all over him already, if not for that dangerous animal he sits. But do not fear his beast, he will not let it hurt you."

Anastasia didn't doubt what Maria said, she never did. She nodded absently and moved toward the middle of the camp, where the strangers had stopped—next to the largest campfire. Ivan sat there and had come to his feet at the intrusion, which was why the blond Englishman was addressing him in his demands, which she heard as she approached.

"You people are trespassing on my land. I will allow that you might not have been aware of this, but now that you are, you will have to leave—"

Ivan was quick to interrupt him before his insistence became irreversible, saying, "We have an old woman who is very ill. She cannot travel just yet."

It was an excuse used many times when they had been asked to move on. Little did Ivan know how true it was this time. But the landowner didn't look convinced. He looked about, ready to repeat his demand.

So Anastasia stepped forward to add her plea. "It is my grandmother who is ill, Lord Englishman. She just needs a few days to rest. We will leave your property as we found it, without harm. Please, you must allow us a day or two, so she can recover her strength."

He almost didn't even turn to glance at her, he was frowning so sternly at Ivan, but when he did, his eyes widened slightly, for the barest moment, giving her an indication that he was as surprised by what he saw as she was. His eyes were very green, very intense. She could not look away from them, recognizing the heated emotion that slowly filled them, delighted by it, for it was what she could work with, this passion he did not think to hide.

When he continued to just stare at her, she added, "Come, meet her. Share a bottle of fine Russian vodka or French wine with us. You will see that we are a harmless people with a few unique services that we offer in our travels, some you might even be interested in."

She knew she was being blatantly provocative, knew what service he would think she was offering, knew that was why he nodded and dismounted to follow her, none of which mattered in the greater scheme of things. She had to get him to herself so they could talk, had to make it seem that they were both fascinated with each other so it would be believed that they had instantly fallen in love with each other, and this was the easiest way.

She led him back to her campfire. Maria had risen, was starting to walk away. Anastasia hadn't thought how she might not appear sick at all to the stranger, yet she needn't have worried. She was too used to seeing Maria daily, which was why she hadn't guessed herself how ill she was. But looking at her through a stranger's eyes, she appeared ancient, pale, feeble—tired of living. It wrenched her heart, to see her that way.

"Gran, I have someone for you to meet."

"Not tonight, child, I need to rest."

Anastasia hadn't expected that, especially since she knew Maria hadn't heard what had been said by Ivan's campfire. Yet she realized quick enough that Maria was attempting to give her some needed time alone with the Englishman. She would have stopped her, though, wanted her opinion of the man, which Maria couldn't formulate if she didn't speak to him herself. He changed her mind.

"Let her go," he said abruptly. "I can see she is not well."

Anastasia nodded and indicated one of the plump canvas pillows on the ground for him to sit on. "I will fetch you something to drink—"

"That won't be necessary," he cut in as

he hobbled his horse a few feet away, then joined her. "Sit. I am intoxicated enough by the sight of you."

She couldn't have asked for a better response from him. She still blushed. She simply wasn't used to this game of enticement, wasn't sure how to play it. But she knew it was her only option, the only way that she could possibly get him to marry her.

She joined him by the fire. Close up, he was even more handsome than she had thought. Everything about him, in fact, was pleasing to the eye.

His clothes were elegant, rather than gaudy as some lords favored. The brown coat that came to his knees was embroidered only on the flaps of the pockets and the large cuffs; the wide skirt of it flared around him as he sat. His knee breeches fit snugly and, with one knee raised to rest his arm on, showed how thickly muscled his thighs were.

The gartered stockings were white silk, as was his shirt, though the only evidence of the shirt was in the ruffles that appeared below his wide, turned-back coat cuffs, and the frills of lace down the front of the shirt that formed his jabot. His body-conforming waistcoat was beige brocade, fastened with a long row of gold buttons, left open from hip to thigh to facilitate easy movement.

Many men wore corsets to improve the fit of these long, slim waistcoats—it was quite fashionable to do so—yet she didn't think this one needed to. He was simply too tightly made, too physically fit—too big, but in a muscular way. She didn't think he would allow any excess flesh to get in the way of his superbly tailored look.

He was staring at her again. She was guilty of the same, actually, couldn't seem to help herself. Yet she knew they were being avidly watched. His two companions had been descended upon by the other women. Music had begun to play. One of the women was dancing one of their more provocative dances to entertain them.

But Anastasia was only barely aware of these things occurring in the camp, so thoroughly did the man next to her hold her attention. So she was a bit startled to finally hear his deep voice again.

"You mentioned services. I am interested in what service you, in particular, offer, pretty one."

She knew what he was expecting to hear, knew that he would be disappointed if she told him merely the truth instead, yet she wasn't going to lie to him any more than was absolutely necessary. Actually, she hoped she wouldn't have to lie to him at all, for that wasn't how she wanted their relationship to start. And she knew, suddenly, with the perfect insight that she was gifted with, that they *would* marry. She just wasn't at all sure yet how she was going to bring it about.

The aroma of Maria's stew was very pleasant. Anastasia stirred it for a moment as she considered what to say to the Englishman. The full truth? A partial truth?

She did not want him to think she was a sorceress with magical powers, as some Gypsies were thought to be. Magic frightened some people. Even things that seemed like magic but weren't frightened some people. She was not possessed of any kind of true magic, just a talent that seemed somewhat magical in nature because it was so accurate. The dilemma was, how to explain that to him.

Chapter Fourteen

Christopher had seen Gypsies before, though never this close. Large bands of them came to camp on the outskirts of London occasionally, to ply their numerous trades and entertain those Londoners daring enough to venture into their camps, but he had never gone himself. He had heard many stories, though, about them. Most not so nice.

Generally they were thought to be thieves and exotic prostitutes, but were also possessed of the legitimate skills of tinkering, horse-trading, music, and dancing. They were considered a very happy, carefree people who abhorred the thought of settling down in any one place. To keep a Gypsy from wandering was to whither his soul, or so he had heard.

This band did indeed seem harmless enough. Their camp was orderly, clean. Their music and laughter were not overly loud. They were mostly dark-skinned and very exotic looking. They were all dressed colorfully in bright skirts and kerchiefs, with pale blouses, the men wearing bright sashes. There was much flashing of cheap jewelry, in long, dangling earrings and many rings, chains, and bracelets.

The wench who had caught his interest so thoroughly seemed different from the others, though. She had the long earrings, the many bracelets and rings. Her clothes were just as colorful, her full skirt a bright yellow and blue, her short-sleeved blouse a pale yellow. She had no kerchief tying back her hair, though, which flowed in free, curly abandon down her back and over her shoulders.

It was her eyes, however, that made her so different. They were tilted at a slight, exotic slant, but were of a brilliant cobalt blue. Her skin, too, was much lighter in color, very fair, smooth as ivory.

She was not very tall. Her head would probably not even reach the top of his shoulders. She was slim of build, petite, yet very nicely shaped. Ample breasts pushed against the thin cotton of her blouse. He had seen women more beautiful, but never one as alluring as this one. He had wanted her the moment he clapped eyes on her. That in itself he found utterly amazing, since it had never happened to him before.

She hadn't answered his question yet. Watching her, enjoying doing so, he nearly forget it, until she said, "I am a healer, a seer, a diviner of dreams." Then with a grin, "You do not look sickly, Lord Englishman."

He chuckled at her. "No, I'm hardly that. Nor do I dream often enough to remember any dream in particular for you to divine. As for seeing into my future, you'll have to excuse me, pretty one, but I'm not about to throw money away on something that cannot be proven until some future date when you are long gone from here."

"A smart man." She smiled, clearly not offended. "But I don't see into the future."

"No?" He raised a golden brow at her. "Then what *do* you see, to be a seer?"

"I see people for what they are, and perhaps help them to see themselves in a clearer light, so that they can correct their own faults and be happier with their lot."

He was amused by such fanciful claims. "I know myself well enough."

"Do you?"

She asked it with such meaning that it gave him pause. But he shook off the immediate curiosity that her insinuation aroused. He was not fooled. These people made their living by taking advantage of the ignorant and superstitious. He was neither. And besides, what he wanted from her, she had not mentioned yet.

"I have coins to spend," he told her matter-of-factly. "Surely you must have something else to sell—that I would find of interest?"

That his eyes moved down her body as he said it could leave little doubt of what he wanted from her. A look like that would have insulted a lady. The wench didn't take offense, though, not even a little. She actually smiled, as if she were delighted he was being so blatant in his desire. Which was why her answer confounded him.

"I am not for sale."

He felt poleaxed. That he couldn't have

her had never occurred to him. His emotions rioted; he refused to accept a no where she was concerned.

He had been rendered speechless, which was perhaps why, after a few moments, she thought to add, "Which does not mean you cannot have me—"

"Excellent!" he jumped in, only to have her hold a hand up so she could finish.

"However, you would not like the condition, so it is not worth discussing."

For someone whose emotions had been pretty much dead for a very long time now, Christopher didn't know quite how to handle these extreme ups and downs the Gypsy was dealing him at the moment.

He ended up frowning and his tone was less than pleasant as he demanded, "What condition?"

She sighed. "Why mention it, when you would never agree to it?"

She turned away from him, started to rise, as if to leave. He grabbed her arm to detain her. He *would* have her. But he was suddenly very angry, that she obviously thought teasing him would up the price.

"How much will it cost me?" he bit out.

She blinked at his tone, yet she didn't try to placate his obvious anger, asked merely, "Why must everything have a price, Lord Englishman? You have made a mistake in thinking I am like these other women. Lying with a *Gajo* means nothing to them, is just another means to put food in the kettle."

"And what makes you different?"

"I am only half Gypsy. My father was as noble as yours, if not more so, a princeling in his own country. From him I have different ideals, one of which is that no man will touch me without benefit of marriage. Now do you understand why I say this is not worth discussing? You would not only have to agree to marry me, you would have to convince my grandmother that you are worthy of me, and I do not foresee either occurring. Now, if you will excuse me . . ."

He was not willing to let her go. Marriage to her was absurd, of course, just as she realized it was. A princeling father indeed. Such an outrageous lie. Yet he still wanted her. There had to be another way to have her. He just needed to figure out how, and needed to keep her here and talking to do that.

Which was why he said, "Tell me more about this 'seeing' thing you do."

She did not mince words with him. "Why, when you doubt me?"

He gave her an earnest smile that he hoped would put her at ease again. "So convince me."

She bit her lip for a moment in indecision. It was a luscious-looking lip. She stirred the kettle again. She stirred things in him as well, with each of her sensuous movements. She appeared deep in thought. Then she sat back and looked into his eyes, just stared, for the longest time, and so intently. He got the strangest, fanciful notion that she really was seeing into the darkest reaches of his soul. The suspense almost had him ready to shout.

At last she said in a mild tone, "Very well. You are not a happy man. It is not that anything has made you unhappy. Actually, there is much in your life that could make you happy, it just doesn't."

His ennui was apparently easy to discern. His friends had remarked on it as well, so he was not surprised that she would pretend to "see" this as his problem.

Annoyed that she called "seeing" what was so obvious that anyone could "see" it, he put her on the spot. "Perhaps you know why?"

"Perhaps I do," she replied, and for a moment, compassion filled her eyes, making him distinctly uncomfortable. "It is because you have lost interest in what you used to be interested in, and have found nothing new to take the place. Because of this you have become—disillusioned? Bored? I'm not quite sure, just that something is seriously lacking in your life. Only recently has it begun to bother you. Perhaps it is merely that you have been alone too long, without family. Everyone benefits from the caring involved in family, yet you have been deprived of this. Perhaps it is merely that you have not found a purpose to your life yet."

He knew it was no more than guessing on her part, and yet her guessing was so bloody accurate, it was frightening. He wanted to hear more, and yet he didn't. Actually, what he really wanted to hear was something that would leave no doubt in his mind that she was a charlatan.

"What else do you see?"

She shrugged carelessly. "Minor things that have nothing to do with your well-being and state of mind."

"Such as?"

"Such as, you could be rich, but you don't really care to pursue great wealth."

He raised a brow. "Excuse me? What makes you think I'm not rich?"

"By my standards, you are. By your standards, you are merely comfortably secure. Even your estate manager earns more than you do from what he manages for you."

Christopher went very still. "That is a slanderous remark, wench, that you had better explain this instant. How could you possibly know that?"

She didn't seem even a little alarmed that she had gained his full ire. "I couldn't," she replied simply. "But I could not help but hear a lot about you when I was in Havers today. Because you come here only rarely, when you do come, you are the subject on everyone's lips. Often was your manager mentioned, and how he has been gulling you ever since you first arrived. For some, the opinion is that it is no more than a lord deserves. For others, they have dealt personally with the man and despise him. Two different motives for saying the same thing usually discounts motive and just speaks the truth. And if it was not true, Lord Englishman, you would have laughed it off. Instead, your anger shows that I merely confirm your own suspicions about the man."

"Anything else?" he asked tightly.

She grinned at him. "Yes, but I think I have made you angry enough for one night. Would you care to share our meager dinner?"

"I've eaten, thank you. And I would prefer to get all of the anger out of the way now, to leave room for—other emotions. So do continue dissecting me."

She blushed at mention of those "other" emotions, understanding very well what he meant. This took the edge off his anger, reminding him that he was sitting there in a state of need because of her, and had yet to figure out a way to take care of that need.

"You do not like to draw attention to yourself," she said, "which is why you do not dress foppishly. It's not because you don't like foppish, it's because you know very well how handsome you are, and this already draws more attention than you are comfortable with."

He laughed. He couldn't help it. "How the devil do you come by that conclusion?"

"That you know very well how handsome you are? Any mirror would show you that. That you might like to dress more fashionably, but don't? I see your companions wearing their expensive jewels, their much brighter colors, their patches and wigs, all very stylish. Yet you dress more sedately, wear no jewelry, not even a velvet ribbon around your neck. You hope that eyes will be drawn to them rather than you. This is a futile hope, though. You are simply an extraordinary-looking man."

He blushed. He was thrilled. He was in pain, her words firing his desire even more.

His hand went to her cheek. He couldn't stop himself, he had to touch her. And she didn't try to prevent his doing so. She merely stared at him, yet with such a swirl of emotion in those startling blue eyes that he almost forgot that they were sitting in the open at her campfire, and pulled her into his arms.

"Come home with me tonight, Gypsy," he said huskily. "You won't regret it."

"You have a *Gajo* priest in residence, then, to give his blessing?"

His hand dropped from her. Frustration filled his eyes. "You are saying you *would* marry me?"

"I am saying I want you, too, Lord Englishman, but without the priest's words, I can't have you. It does not get more simple than that."

"Simple?" he all but snorted. "You must know that is impossible, that people from my social stature only marry within their class."

"Yes, I know very well how nobles are governed by the opinions of their peers, which does not leave them free to do as they please. A shame you aren't a common man, Lord Englishman. They have more freedom than you."

"And how free are you, to not do as you want?" he shot back in a frustrated tone. "Or did you not just tell me that you want me?"

"I can't deny that. Yet I am restricted by my own morals, rather than the opinions of others. If you must know, my own people would be scandalized if I were to marry you. Ironically, you would not be an acceptable mate for me, for you are not one of us. Would I let that influence me? No. Only one's heart should matter in these things. Yet mine will not let me go to a man who will not be mine to keep. I do not hold myself that cheaply."

"Then we have nothing further to say." He stood up and tossed a few coins into her lap. "For your insight," he said with a measure of derision. "Too bad you couldn't 'see' a way for us to be together."

"But I did," she replied sadly. "Too bad you don't want me enough to keep me."

Chapter Fifteen

Too bad you don't want me enough to keep me.

Oddly enough, Christopher did want her that much. He realized it about noon the next day, when she simply would not get out of his mind. He couldn't get any work done for thinking of her. He rudely ignored his friends as well. They'd had a very good time last evening, a good time that included getting from the other Gypsy wenches what he'd been denied himself. Not that he begrudged them that. It was just driving him crazy, that he hadn't been as lucky.

He started drinking in the early afternoon, in an effort to dull his disappointment. It didn't really help. What it did do was make it much easier for him to decide to make the Gypsy his mistress. Surely that would satisfy her "mine to keep" morals, wouldn't it?

It was just barely dark when he rode to the Gypsy camp again. He didn't bring David or Walter with him this time, didn't even tell them where he was going, since he had every intention of bringing the Gypsy home with him, yet he didn't want his friends to know how completely she had bewitched him, to the point of wanting to set her up in London where she would always be available to him.

She wasn't at the campfire where he had left her last night. The old woman was there, though. He tethered his horse near her. No one came to question what he was doing there, probably because they didn't want to know if he was there to evict them again.

"I'm looking for your granddaughter, madame," he said without preamble.

She looked up at him, her eyes crinkling as she smiled. "Of course you are. Here, sit, and give me your hand," she said, patting the pillow next to her.

He sat, but he wasn't sure why he gave her his hand. She held it loosely in her gnarled fingers; there was no strength in her grip. Her eyes closed briefly, then opened to stare into his. It was the strangest sensation, feeling as if your soul were being touched.

Fanciful. He shouldn't have drunk so much today, shouldn't have brought a full bottle of rum with him either, as if he needed extra courage to ask the Gypsy to be his mistress. Actually, he wasn't at all sure what her answer would be, and really just wanted his senses deadened somewhat, in case she turned him down.

"You are a very fortunate man," the old woman said to him at last. "What I give to you will bring you happiness for the rest of your life."

"And what is that?"

She was smiling at him again. "You will know when the time is right."

More nonsense. These people thrived on being mysterious. He supposed it was part of their allure. But he was impatient to see the girl again.

"Where is your granddaughter?"

"She has been asked to dance. She is preparing herself now. It won't be long."

Even another minute was too long as far as he was concerned. His impatience was incredible. After forcing himself to stay away all day, he refused to be put off, now that he was here.

"Yes, but *where* is she preparing? I merely wish to speak with her."

The old Gypsy chuckled. "And so you shall, but after she dances. She doesn't need the distraction you present, when the dance requires her full concentration. Patience, *Gajo,* you will get what you want."

"Will I? When what I want is her?"

He shouldn't have said that to her grandmother, of all people. It was beyond tactless. The one pitfall of too much drink was a loose tongue, and he'd just stumbled over it. But it was too late to take it back now. Fortunately, she didn't appear offended.

She merely nodded and asked in her heavily accented English, "You have one of your religious men ready to give his blessing, then?"

That nonsense again? "Preposterous. I'm an English lord, madame."

"So? She's a Romany princess, as noble in her birthland as you are in yours. And if you want her, you will have to marry her."

"I have come up with an acceptable alternative," he told her stiffly.

"Have you indeed? One she will find more favorable than marrying that Gypsy there, whose father is our *barossan* and has already paid her bride-price?"

Christopher tensed, filling with a rage the likes of which he'd never felt before. "Which Gypsy?"

"The handsome one there leaning against that tree—who will be dancing the *tanana* with her tonight. It is very, very rare for a *Gajo* to ever witness the *tanana.* You are blessed, English, to have come at the right time to see it."

That "dancing with her" seemed to have some significant meaning that he couldn't figure out in his drink-befuddled state. He did find the man she had waved toward, and saw him leaving the tree. Following the direction he headed, he saw the girl who'd been haunting his mind and drew in his breath at her sensual beauty.

She wore a low-cut, off-the-shoulder

white blouse, the deep scoop of it bordered with a lacy ruffle, dotted with tiny gold sequins. Her full skirt was a shiny gold, and glittered even more with large gold bangles sewn about the hem. Her only jewelry was the long earrings that flashed and tinkled with her slightest movement. A shawl-like white scarf, also dotted with gold sequins, draped over her gleaming black hair and down her sides.

She was shining from head to toe. She was beautiful. She didn't notice that Christopher was there. She was staring at the Gypsy as her arms lifted, beginning the dance . . .

The young man was indeed handsome, tall, slim, graceful in his leaps and movements. Christopher felt too big and utterly clumsy in comparison. The dance was mesmerizing. They never lost eye contact with each other, no matter how frenzied the tempo and movements became. It was a dance of passion, of temptation, of two lovers flirting, teasing, denying, offering, promising . . .

"He can't have her. I forbid it," Christopher said adamantly, proving just how intoxicated he was.

Not surprisingly, the old woman laughed at him. "You can't forbid it, English. All you can do is prevent it by marrying her yourself."

"I *can't* marry her, madame."

A long, drawn-out sigh. "Then stop thinking you can have her, enjoy the dance, and go home. We will move on in the morning."

He hadn't taken his eyes off of the girl since she had appeared, nor did he now. But the old woman's words caused an unexpected panic he couldn't quite control. They'd leave—*she* would leave? He'd never see her again? Unacceptable. She *would* agree to be his mistress. He'd buy her anything she wanted, give her anything—short of a marriage license. How could she not agree?

Yet as much as he wanted to believe that money would solve this for him, that couldn't be depended on when dealing with a people so different from his own. He was out of his element. Who but foreigners would think that he could just *marry* her, just like that, ignoring the fact that he was a titled lord and she was a common vagrant? Well, not so common. Well, utterly beautiful, utterly desirable, but that was beside the point. It simply couldn't be done.

Why not?

The question startled him. He needed another drink. That, at least, was easily done, and he pulled the bottle of rum out of his wide coat pocket, opened it, and tipped it to his lips, still without taking his eyes from her.

She was desire. She was passion. She danced like an angel. She danced like a wanton. God, he wanted her. He had never wanted anything as much as he wanted her. She made him feel again. It had been so long since his emotions had been this alive. He had to have her. No matter the cost, he had to have her . . .

Chapter Sixteen

The groan woke him. Christopher couldn't figure out where it had come from until he heard it again and realized he was the one groaning. His head was splitting apart. A bloody hangover, and no more than he deserved, he supposed, for drinking rum, of all things. It certainly wasn't his normal libation, but he'd wanted something strong yesterday, and there had been nothing else left in the house—which he would see about rectifying first thing today.

"I can fix that for you."

The voice was lightly accented, soft as a whisper. He turned to see who it belonged to. He wasn't surprised to see that it was *her,* lying on the pillow next to him, smiling at him. Ann, Anna, no, Anastasia, yes, that was the name he had finally got from her at some point last night, though he couldn't remember just when.

"Fix what?"

"The pain you're experiencing from your overindulgence last night."

"Oh, that?" He winced as another pain shot through his temples. "Think nothing of it. If you'll just come a little closer and let me hold you, the pleasure of that will make me forget all about my aching head."

She touched his brow gently. "No it won't, but it's sweet of you to say so."

She moved closer anyway, pressing to his side and resting her head on his chest. He sighed blissfully as he realized she was quite naked under the sheet. Whatever had happened last night between them—why the deuce couldn't he remember?—he had little doubt that he had enjoyed it.

"So you agreed?" he said with a good deal of male satisfaction as he ran a hand through her soft hair. "Knew you would, though I'm damned if I can remember it."

"You insisted, if you must know."

"I did? Well, good for me."

She chuckled. It was a husky sound that provoked a quick response in his lower regions. Amazing, how easily she could make him want her.

"Not recalling the best part of the evening leaves me feeling distinctly—unsatisfied," he told her with some chagrin. "But I'm ready to have a go at it again, so I can remember it this time."

Her head lifted so she could look at him. Her lovely eyes held humor, but tenderness as well. "Again? I hate to disappoint you, Christoph, but the moment your head touched that pillow last night, you were fast asleep. You didn't even stir once when I undressed you, and that was no easy task, as big and heavy as you are. A cannon could have gone off in this room, and you wouldn't have—"

"I get the idea," he grouched. "Bloody hell, I drank *that* much?"

She nodded with a grin. "You really are quite funny deep in your cups. You don't slur your speech. You don't stagger or sway in your movements. You don't appear intoxicated at all. But the things you say—I really doubt you would say them if you had a clear mind."

"Such as?"

"Oh, such as when you told me I would *never* dance again. So silly, of course I will—whenever you ask me to. And when you tossed me up onto your horse and told me to stay there while you killed Nicolai."

His eyes widened. "I didn't, did I?"

"No, you got distracted, trying to find a weapon in one of your pockets, then finally couldn't remember what you were looking for."

He grimaced. "Never again. If I ever see another bottle of rum, I'll—"

"Yes, I know, you'll break it over your head before you drink it."

"I wouldn't go *that* far."

She chuckled. "I didn't think so, but that *is* what you said last night."

The sound of her humor again stirred him. He pulled her farther up his chest, so that her mouth was within reach of his. His eyes locked with hers. He had no doubt she would recognize the desire she could see in his.

"So we haven't made love yet?" he said huskily.

"No, nor will we," she said matter-of-factly, "not until I rid you of that awful headache I know you are suffering. When I make love to you, Christoph, I want you to feel only pleasure. I did not exaggerate when I told you I was skilled at healing. The knowledge of herb lore has been in my family for many generations. This will not take long."

He was beset by several different emotions at once, hotter desire when she spoke of making love *to* him, acute disappointment when she left the bed, abrupt awe as he was treated to a full view of her nakedness.

She behaved as if it were a perfectly normal thing to do, to walk about unclothed. Not a bit of self-consciousness or embarrassment did she show. Nor was she proudly flaunting that luscious body before him, though she certainly had reason to. She simply went to a cloth satchel that was hers, rummaged through it until she found what she was looking for, then looked about the room until she spotted what else she needed—glasses and several decanters, one that was replenished with fresh water each day.

She opened each decanter to sniff it, then, surprising, chose the brandy to sprinkle some crushed herbs into. Stirring it briskly with her finger, which she then sucked clean, much to Christopher's horror—what that did to his already stiff condition was quite painful—she came back to the bed and handed him the glass.

There was barely a half inch of the golden spirits in the glass, made murky, though, by the powdered herb, which had him staring at it with a frown. "Why the brandy rather than the water?"

"Because the cure isn't very pleasant tasting, and the brandy will mask the taste. Drink it. You will feel much better in only, oh, fifteen minutes or so. Just enough time for me to take a quick bath."

The thought of her in his large tub had him gulping down her concoction to set it aside. "I'll join you—if you don't mind."

"I don't mind." She smiled down at him. "If you will promise to keep your hands to yourself until you are feeling no more pain."

He sighed. "Never mind, I'll suffer here—er, wait here for you."

She nodded, leaned over to kiss his brow, then paused to whisper by his ear,

"Good things come to those who wait, Christoph."

It was on the tip of his tongue to point out to her that his name wasn't that for- eign-sounding Christoph, but he chose in- stead to savor the sight of those magnificent breasts that had come so close to his mouth when she leaned over him. He heard the door to the bathroom close and sighed again. But it wasn't long before he was fantasizing about her in that decadent bathroom.

It was the only room in the entire house that didn't fit the current decor and had been a complete surprise to him, on his first inspection of the estate. It was as if some puritan of the last century had deco- rated the house, but that single room had been hidden from them and so left intact. It was ancient Roman in design, huge, with a sunken tub that could easily fit six adults, entered by marble steps, surrounded by Grecian columns. Naked gold cherubs formed the waterspouts on the tub and the ornate sink.

He *would* bathe with her in there, and before they left for London. London . . .

which reminded him, where the deuce was he going to keep her until he could find a suitable place for her? The servants in his town house couldn't be trusted not to gossip about her. Here in the country it hardly mattered; servant gossip didn't travel that far. But in London it certainly did, and he didn't care to have it run through the mills that he'd been bewitched by a Gypsy, despite the fact that it was absolutely true.

The door opened. She came back into the room as naked as when she'd left it. She came straight to the bed. She kneeled on it, threw back the sheet, then kneeled over him. He sucked in his breath at her boldness as she settled herself to sit on his loins. Her hip-length hair, which had graced her sides, curled on his belly in front of her.

"How is your headache?" she asked matter-of-factly, as if he weren't mesmerized by her actions.

"What headache?"

She smiled at that answer. "Any regrets, Christoph?"

He chuckled and moved his hips against her. "You must be joking."

She rolled her eyes. "I mean beyond

what we are about to do. I know I can make you happy. I just wonder if you regret what fate has dealt you. I certainly do not."

He reached up to caress her cheek. "I don't think you realize how much you have already done for me. You were more accurate than I care to admit, in what you saw in me. I had become a dead shell. You've brought me back to life."

Her smile became brilliant. "We will be good for each other." She braced her hands on the bed at his shoulders to lean over him and whisper against his lips, "Very good."

He groaned, his arms going around her, pulling her down to feel all of her against him. And her lips, he captured those, too, his mouth closing with a voracious demand on hers. He felt her tense. It was too much passion all at once, yet he couldn't seem to slow down. It was as if he'd waited years and years for this one moment, this one woman, and there was no stopping him now that both were his.

But she stopped him. She forced herself out of his hold, and in his momentary surprise, she cupped his cheeks and ordered sharply, "Listen to me, Christoph. I will not let you hurt me because you are so intoxicated with passion that you are not thinking about what you are doing. Do you forget this is my first time with a man? Some other time we can do this swiftly, if that is your wish, but not this time. This time you will have a care for what you must break. I am prepared for the pain, but only you can lessen its impact. Or does it not matter to you if I suffer more?"

"Of course it matters," he said automatically.

Yet he was still reeling over her words. Good God, how could she be a virgin and be as bold as she'd been? Yet the truth would be discovered within moments, so this couldn't be a pretense on her part.

"You are awful brazen for a virgin," he pointed out, rather tactlessly, he realized too late.

But she laughed, rather than taking offense. "We are going to spend the rest of our lives together. For what reason would I conceal anything from you? I am yours, Christoph. It would be silly for me to hide myself from you, would it not?"

I am yours. Strangely enough, hearing her say that filled him with tenderness. He rolled them over, so that he was the one leaning over her. He kissed her, gently this time. There was much to be said for savoring the moment.

She tasted heavenly. Her lips parted easily for him, pulled on his tongue as he sent it exploring. His hand moved over her firm breast. She arched upward, filling his hand completely. He nearly laughed in delight. A wanton virgin, what more could a man ask for?

"You will tell me, then, when you are ready?" he asked huskily.

"I think . . . you will know," she gasped out.

So he would. He smiled, continuing his exploration. Her skin was silken smooth, warm. He found himself caressing her reverently, marveling at her perfect shape, her softness, her reactions to his touch. He was hard, aching to be inside her, yet he was so fascinated by her that it was the sweetest bliss, watching her experience lovemaking for the first time. She shivered, she groaned, she thrust against his touch. She made him feel as if he were experiencing lovemaking for the first time as well.

And he did indeed know when she was ready. He was careful of his weight when he moved over her to settle between her thighs, and even more careful in entering her. The barrier was there as she'd claimed, and he did more teeth-gritting than she as he sundered it open. Her gasp was loud, but no more than a gasp. His kiss soothed her further.

He gave her a few moments to recover from the discomfort, didn't continue until she began returning his kiss. Her passion reignited, he slid the rest of the way into her depths, slowly, exquisitely, until at last she fit all of him. It was nearly more than he could bear without losing control, such tight heat gripping him, so much pleasure, yet he managed to hold off the final bliss, to withdraw and begin a gentle thrusting that she could tolerate. Yet it was soon apparent that she was beyond the need for moderation, and one deep thrust sent them both on that glorious ride to fruition.

Chapter Seventeen

Christopher had never realized just how pleasant it could be, to simply hold a woman close to him and savor the feel of her warm body. He supposed he'd never really taken the time before to find out, always impatient to either sleep or be off about his business, once he finished satisfying his needs. Then, too, he'd never "kept" a mistress before, or brought one into his own bed.

Not that he hadn't had many mistresses over the years, but they'd had their own abodes, their own agendas separate from his, and the typical arrangement with these types of mistresses was that they'd merely agree to accommodate each other exclusively for a time. They'd cost him no more than the occasional expensive trinket.

Anastasia, now, would be completely "kept." He'd be supplying her with a home where he could visit her, servants to see to her comfort, clothes, food, as well as the expensive trinkets. She was going to be costly. She was most definitely worth it.

"You sound famished," she said when they'd both heard his belly rumble for the third time.

"Perhaps because I am," he replied lazily, still in no hurry to get up. "Come to think of it, don't recall having dinner last night—bloody hell, it's no wonder that rum went right to my head. Any idea what time it is?"

"Quite late, midmorning at least."

He chuckled. "You call that late?"

"When you're used to rising with the dawn, yes, that's very late."

He smiled. "There'll be no reason for you to rise that early anymore."

"I happen to like the dawn, to watch the sunrise. Don't you?"

"Hmmm, never thought about it—actually, don't recall seeing too many sunrises. Sunsets are more in line with my habits."

"I think you'll enjoy the dawn with me, Christoph," she predicted.

"I *know* you'll enjoy sunsets with me," he countered.

"And why can't we enjoy both?"

He sat up to look down at her. "You aren't thinking of changing my habits, are you? And why do you persist in calling me Christoph? Didn't I tell you last night that my name was Christopher?"

"You did. Kit, too, you said your friends call you. But I happen to like Christoph much better. It sounds more lyrical to my ears. Consider it an endearment."

"Must I?"

She chuckled and rolled to the side of the bed, then headed for her clothes. "I think we must feed you immediately. Empty bellies lead to grouchiness."

He blinked, then grinned to himself. She was right, of course. There was nothing wrong with her having a pet name for him. And besides, when she sashayed about the room naked like that, he simply couldn't find anything really worth complaining about.

He got up to dress as well. When he

finished and glanced at her again, it was to find that she was wearing that flashy dancing costume from last night, which would draw more attention to her than he would like.

"Have you nothing else to wear?" he asked.

"You didn't exactly give me the opportunity to pack last night, Christoph. All I have is my satchel, which my grandmother tossed up to me just before you sent that mad stallion of yours galloping out of the camp."

He grimaced with the reminder that he'd been less than gentlemanly last night. "I'll take you back today to collect your things—and perhaps to town to buy something more . . . normal looking."

She raised a brow at his choice of words. "You think my clothes are not normal?"

"Well, certainly they are." His tone turned conciliatory. "It is just, they are . . . well . . ."

He couldn't come up with an appropriate word that wouldn't insult her. She supplied some for him, and it wasn't difficult to see that she *was* insulted.

"Common perhaps? Peasantlike? Suitable only for Gypsy vagabonds?"

"There is no need for you to take offense, Anastasia. Your clothes were perfectly fine for the life you were living on the road. But you'll be living differently from now on. It's as simple as that."

She was frowning now, not at all placated. "Are you going to have trouble, Christoph, dealing with what I am?"

"What you are?"

"That I'm a Gypsy?"

"Half Gypsy, or so you've claimed."

She waved that aside. "I was raised as a Gypsy, not as a Russian. I may not think or do exactly as most Gypsies, but I am still one of them."

He came over to her and put his arms around her. "We are not having our first fight."

"We aren't?"

"No, we aren't. I forbid it."

She leaned back to stare into his eyes. "I will make some allowances to accommodate you. You must do the same for me.

In such a way we can come to agree on everything in the end. Fair enough?"

"You have a unique way of looking at things that I think I can get quite used to. For right now, shall we agree to raid the kitchen?"

"If that is what it takes to obtain some breakfast, certainly." She waved her arm toward the door with a flourish and a bow. "After you—Lord Englishman."

He rolled his eyes and pushed her in front of him so he could swat her backside playfully. "No more of that. Christoph will most definitely do."

She giggled. "If you insist."

Chapter Eighteen

It was too much to hope, really, that they would continue to get along perfectly, yet a few days or weeks wouldn't have been too much to expect—rather than the time it took them to walk downstairs that morning.

Thinking back on it, Christopher allowed that he could have been more tactful. But guarding his words was simply not his habit, especially among his friends. Who else, after all, would he feel like bragging to about his splendid acquisition than his closest friends?

Walter and David were that, but he could have wished they hadn't appeared in the hallway below just as he was coming down the stairs, Anastasia's hand in his, though she was a few steps behind him.

And both men couldn't help but notice them, of course, when that flashy gold skirt of hers was like a beacon in the dark.

"What's this?" David asked, eyeing Anastasia, though his question was for Christopher. "So *that's* where you went off to last night?"

"Taking her back to her camp?" Walter surmised, then with a grin, "We'll come along."

"Not exactly," Christopher corrected. "I'll take her later to collect her belongings, but she'll be staying with me from now on. She's agreed to let me keep her."

"Oh, I say, d'you think that's wise, Kit?" David asked. "She's not exactly typical mistress material."

Anastasia yanked her hand out of Christopher's at that point, but with David's remark in his mind, he barely noticed. "What has typical got to do with it?" he asked. "I've had 'typical,' David, and lose interest in it in a matter of days, same as you do. Which certainly won't be the case with my Anna here. Besides, I didn't ask her to be my mistress to introduce her to society, so it hardly matters whether she's typical or unique, now does it?"

"Er, not to be the bearer of dire tidings, old chum," Walter remarked. "But I'd say your Anna is about to take your head off— metaphorically speaking."

Christopher spun around just in time to receive a resounding slap across his cheek and watch Anastasia hike her skirt and run back up the stairs. "What the devil was that for?" he called after her.

But she didn't stop, and a moment later he heard the door slam shut to his room. The entire house likely heard it, actually.

"Bloody hell," he muttered.

Behind him, David was tactfully coughing into his hand, but Walter was outright chuckling. "No, indeed, nothing typical about that a'tall. Though it might help you to know, Kit, that she began frowning as soon as David introduced the subject of mistresses."

"Sure, blame it on me," David grumbled.

Christopher ignored his friends and marched back to his room. The door wasn't locked against him. He found Anastasia stuffing a few things that had been left out of her satchel back into it.

He closed the door behind him and leaned back against it. He wasn't angry, but he was certainly annoyed, and not just a little confused. A mistress had no conceivable reason to get upset at being called a mistress.

"Just what do you think you're doing?" he demanded. "And why the devil did you hit me?"

She paused long enough to glare at him. "I did not take you for a fool, Christopher Malory. Do not pretend to be one now."

"I beg your pardon?" he replied stiffly.

"As well you should," she snapped. "But you are *not* forgiven!"

"I wasn't asking to be. If I said anything wrong, I'm bloody well damned if I know what it was. So why don't you tell me what you objected to, then perhaps—*perhaps,* mind you—I will apologize."

Her face flushed furiously. "I take it back, *Gajo,* you are a fool." She marched toward him. "Get out of my way. I am going home."

He didn't move away from the door. He

did grab her shoulders to keep her in front of him, though he refrained, just barely, from shaking her.

"You aren't going anywhere until you at least explain yourself. You owe me that much."

Her lovely cobalt eyes flared. "I owe you nothing after what you just did!"

"*What* did I do?"

"You not only let those men insult me, but you stood there and did exactly the same thing. How could you speak of me like that? How could you?!"

He sighed at that point. "Those are my closest friends, Anastasia. Do you think I wouldn't be proud to show you off to them?"

"Show me off? I am not a toy. You didn't purchase me. And I am *not* your mistress!"

"The devil you aren't," he snapped, but then he paused and frowned. "Don't tell me I forgot to ask you last night. That's why I went back to your camp. Why else would you be here, unless I asked you and you accepted?"

"Oh, you asked me," she said in a soft, furious whisper. "And this was my answer."

For the second time, she slapped him.

His face turned quite red this time, and not just from the slap. *Now* he was angry.

"Do *not* hit me again, Anna. It was a natural assumption for me to make, that you had agreed to be my mistress, particularly since I woke up to find you lying naked in my bed. Blister it, you even *said* you agreed. I distinctly remember you saying so this morning. What the devil did you agree to, if not that?"

"You have only to recall what I told you was the only way you could have me, and you'd have your answer. I'm not your mistress, I'm your wife!"

"The devil you are!"

It was probably because he looked so horrified that she shoved her way past him and out the door. That he was utterly horrified was why he stood there in complete bemusement, rather than try to stop her. He just couldn't believe that, drunk or not, he would so totally ignore the strictures of his class. A marquis did *not* marry a common Gypsy, well, not so common, but still a Gypsy, well, half Gypsy, but still . . . it just wasn't done.

She was obviously lying, a ruse to trick

him into thinking that he'd married her, and she'd been able to do it because he got so sotted with drink last night that he couldn't remember what he'd done. Of all the bloody nerve, and especially when he only had to demand some proof and she'd have to fess up that she'd lied, since there wouldn't be any proof. He would have thought she was more intelligent than that, to think she could get away with it. Some of his fast-rising rage stemmed from disappointment in her.

He went after her. She'd already left the house. He just barely spotted that bright skirt disappearing into the woods quite some distance away. It was too far for him to catch up to her on foot, though, so he ran to his stable.

She was no more than halfway to her camp when his stallion came galloping up behind her and was yanked to a rearing stop a bit in front of her. She ignored him and the beast and continued her march, merely veering around him. It was an easy matter to move the horse in front of her again, and again, until she got the idea and stopped.

He extended a hand to her, to lift her up. When she just stared at it, he explained, "I took you away from your camp last night, I'll return you to it today. It's the gentlemanly thing to do."

She snorted. "How convenient, to play the gentleman only when it suits you."

That was a serious insult that had him retaliating in kind. "I wouldn't expect a Gypsy to grasp the intricacies of the nobility."

She raised a brow at him. "Is that a roundabout way of saying that the intricacies of common courtesy are beyond the grasp of the nobility?"

He blinked. "I beg your pardon?"

"Don't bother. I already mentioned that you won't be forgiven, didn't I?"

He gritted his teeth. "That's a blasted phrase that requests an explanation when delivered in that tone, *not* a request for forgiveness!"

"Is it indeed? When a simple 'what' would have gotten the point across without causing confusion? Another one of those subtle 'intricacies' understood only by you lordly types, I suppose?"

He rolled his eyes and said in a weary tone, "You are being obtuse, Anastasia."

She matched his tone and added a sigh. "And you are being dense, Lord Englishman, or have you not grasped yet that I have nothing further to say to you?"

He stiffened. "Very well, but before we part, I would like to know how you thought you could possibly convince me that I had married you."

"Convince you?" She laughed unpleasantly. "There is probably a paper in your coat pocket with our signatures on it, unless you managed to lose it last night. But then you could always ask the Reverend Biggs—I believe that was the name he supplied. You threatened to beat him to within an inch of his life if he didn't marry us, and poor man, he quite believed you. So do whatever needs doing to unmarry us. There will be no need to inform me when it is done, since I have no doubt whatsoever that you will see to it posthaste."

She was able to walk away from him again, because again, she'd rendered him quite beyond speech.

Chapter Nineteen

She wasn't going to cry. He was an insensitive beast, an arrogant wretch, and as he might put it, a "bloody" snob. But she wasn't going to cry. She had seen his confusion and wanted to help him. She had seen his pain and wanted to heal it. She had seen his emptiness and wanted to fill him with happiness instead. But she hadn't seen that he could be so foolish as to put the opinions of others before his own needs. She hadn't seen that he would sacrifice his own happiness because "it just wasn't done."

It was appalling, to have been so wrong about him, and worse, to let her own emotions take over. Her heart wasn't supposed to get so involved—yet. She shouldn't be devastated that he couldn't stand the thought of being married to her, when she'd known from the start that he felt that way—when he wasn't drunk. Drunk, he let his heart guide him. Drunk, nothing was going to stand in the way of what he wanted, certainly not his silly "it just wasn't done."

Anastasia entered the camp blindly, her mind too filled with misery to notice Nicolai until he caught her arm and painfully jerked her around to face him. His fingers would leave bruises. She was always left with bruises whenever he touched her.

"Where did you spend the night?" he demanded.

She should have been wise enough to lie, especially since he looked quite furious, but with her emotions in such turmoil already, it was defiance that reared its ugly head. Chin raised, she answered, "With my husband."

The slap was not unexpected. Even the brutality of it that sent her to the ground was no more than typical of Nicolai. Anastasia tossed her hair out of the way and glared up at him balefully.

"Perhaps you did not hear me correctly, Nico. I was with my husband, the *Gajo* I married last night, the *Gajo* who will see you end up in an English prison if you ever lay a hand on me again."

He looked suitably uncertain, as she had hoped he would. He even paled slightly at the mention of prison, since most Gypsies would rather die than be locked up for any length of time. Yet he still doubted her, and with good reason.

"You are promised to me!" he reminded her. "You would not dare marry another."

"Promised to you, but not by me, never by me. You were never my choice, Nico, nor would I have ever agreed to marry you. I would have chosen anyone other than you, whom we both know I hate. Yet I chose for love instead, yes, love, a concept you know nothing about!"

He would have hit her again if she weren't lying on the ground, out of his immediate reach. And they had gathered an audience, not close, but just about everyone in the camp was listening and watching, including his father—including Maria, who was approaching them as fast as her old bones allowed. She did not usually wit-

ness Anastasia's confrontations with Nicolai. This one had her enraged.

Nicolai saw her coming and stiffened.
There wasn't a one among them, even his
father, who wasn't just a little afraid of Maria. Her insights were *too* accurate, as were
her curses. And she *was* their luck. You did
not take chances with guaranteed luck.

Yet he was too furious to consider any
of that for more than a moment, and raised
a hand to ward her off. "This does not con-
cern you, old woman."

Her answer was to throw gold coins at
him. Each one hit him squarely, each hit a
different spot, each stung worse than it
should have, coming from such a weak-
armed throw.

"There is your bride-price," Maria spat
contemptuously. "My granddaughter is now
nothing to you, a stranger, and you will treat
her as such, keeping your eyes off her,
keeping your hands off her."

"You can't do this!" he growled.

"It is done. Even if she wanted you, I
would not let you have her. You are not
worthy of a dog, much less a woman. Your

father is to be pitied, having such a son as you."

"Your words are worse than harsh, Maria," Ivan blustered, coming to stand next to them. "I understand anger prompts them, but—"

"Not anger, Ivan, but the unfortunate truth," Maria interrupted. "No one else dares to speak it to you, but I do. The dying know no fear."

He had heard enough before he joined them to pale at the significance of those last words. "No! We cannot lose you both."

"You have no choice this time. You cannot keep Anna when her heart leads her elsewhere. To try would bring no benefit, would instead bring disaster. But you have no one to blame but yourself, Ivan. Had you taught Nicolai better, had you curbed his cruel tendencies, she might have come to love him, instead of hating him."

Ivan was blushing furiously after that, yet he couldn't dispute such brutal truths, when Nicolai was indeed a disappointment to him. Yet their good fortune was at stake here, their incredibly long reign of luck, which he could not bear to see ended.

"Does it mean nothing, that we have always taken care of you Stephanoffs, that you have always had your home with us?" he said, trying to use guilt to reach her. "Where has your loyalty gone?"

"Loyalty?" Maria scoffed. "You lost mine years ago when you threatened me, Ivan, over my daughter's leaving. Or did you think this old woman would ever forget that? What you have had since then is mere apathy on my part, since there is no other band that I cared to join. But we come again to the crossroads, of one of mine needing to go her own way, and she will *not* be hindered in this."

"Maria—"

"No!" she cut in sharply. "There is no more to say, except this. I have given my life in service to you and yours, but it is over. If you don't want me dying with a curse on my lips that will follow you until the end of your days, you will bid your farewells to my granddaughter and wish her happiness in the path she has chosen. Good fortune will still be yours as long as you are wise enough not to interfere with love."

It was a sop for him to salvage his pride and walk away with dignity. This he did with a curt nod to first her, then Anastasia. His son had no dignity to begin with, however, so it was not surprising that he spat on the ground at Maria's feet before he stalked off.

Anastasia had gotten to her feet when Maria arrived. She put her arm around her shoulders now to help her back to their wagon. She could feel her weakness, hear her labored breath, now that the confrontation was over.

"You strained yourself," she scolded. "I thought we agreed that I would handle that."

"You would deny me my last great fury?"

Anastasia sighed. "No, of course not. Did you at least enjoy it?"

"Immensely, child, immensely. Now, where is this husband of yours? Why isn't he with you?"

At which point, considering what she must answer, Anastasia promptly burst into tears.

Chapter Twenty

It was still morning, but Anastasia had put her grandmother to bed. There was very little life's essence left in Maria now. Anastasia could feel none as she sat there and held her cold hand.

A death vigil. She knew that was what this was. Sir William shared it with her, standing silently behind her, his hand on her shoulder. It was all she could do to assure Maria that she would be fine, when she had no idea if that would be so, when she was trying to deal with her grief as well. Yet it all needed saying.

"He holds himself unaccountable for what he did while he was drunk last night," Anastasia said in answer to why the marquis wasn't there with her. "He thought I agreed to be his mistress, and he was delighted with that assumption. He refused to believe he'd married me instead. He actually thought I would lie about such a thing."

"So you think he didn't really want you?" Maria asked. "After meeting him, I know this isn't so."

"He wants me, just not for his wife. Which is fine. I aspired too high, apparently, to the likes of him. I will be wiser next time."

"Next time?" Maria chuckled softly. "There will be no next time."

Anastasia misunderstood. "Then I will remain without a husband. It makes no difference to me," she tried to assure Maria. "The English lord, he served the purpose we needed. I am no longer promised to Nicolai because of him. For that, I am grateful."

The old woman smiled. "You have a husband. You will keep that husband."

"I don't want him now," Anastasia tried to insist, though she was never very good at lying, and particularly to Maria, who could unravel a lie so easily.

"You do."

"Really, Gran, I don't. And besides, as

soon as he finds proof that we married, other than my word, which he would *not* believe, he'll have the marriage dissolved quicker than it takes to blink."

"He won't."

Anastasia sighed, but then chuckled wryly. "Very well, I am sure you have good reason to be so stubborn about this. Why won't he divorce me?"

"Because you showed him light, daughter of my heart. He won't go back to the darkness that was his before he met you. He is not a complete fool, though it may seem otherwise to you just now. It may take him a while to figure this out. You need only wait, and be prepared to forgive him when he comes to his senses."

"Or nudge him a bit, to hurry him along," Sir William suggested.

Anastasia swung around in surprise at the Englishman's unexpected remark. "I would not ask you to speak with him, William."

"Nor would I be so presumptuous," he said in his stiff English way. "He *is* a marquis, after all, while I'm merely a lowly knight."

"Then how would you go about nudging a marquis?" Maria questioned.

William grinned, somewhat conspiratorially. "I could take her to London, dress her in fine gowns, introduce her as my niece. It would show that young pup that appearances and origins mean very little in the end, that happiness is all that really matters."

"You would do that for us?"

"I would do anything for you, Maria," William replied softly.

She reached for his hand, brought it to her leathery cheek. "Perhaps I will ignore those handsome young angels after all, *Gajo*."

He beamed at her. "I will fend them off when I get there, if you forget."

She made a semblance of a smile. Her eyes closed slowly, the light gone out of them.

Her voice was but a whisper now. "I leave her in your care, then. Guard well this treasure of mine. And thank you . . . for letting me go in peace."

Her breathing stopped, as did her heartbeat. Anastasia stared at her in shocked silence, yet inside she wailed, she keened, she futilely beat her breast, and it changed nothing. Her grandmother was dead.

"Maria wouldn't want you to cry, lass, but sometimes that is the only way to get the pain out."

This was said kindly and with a catch; William was crying silently himself. Yet he was right, on both counts. Maria wouldn't want her to grieve, wouldn't want either of them to grieve. She'd said as much.

Anastasia began to cry, not for her grandmother, who had found peace from her pain, who really wouldn't want tears shed for her after she'd lived such a full life, but for her own loneliness . . .

Sir William helped her dig the grave. She had had many offers from the stronger of the men to do this, but had refused all but the Englishman's help. The others had respected Maria, were in awe of her, but they hadn't loved her.

By custom, everything that Maria had owned was buried with her or destroyed. Even the old wagon was put to the torch. But Anastasia defied Gypsy tradition in two things. She let Maria's horses go free, rather than slaughter them as was usually done whenever it was assured the legal authorities wouldn't interfere. And she kept the ring that had been given to Maria by her first husband.

"The first was the one I most loved," Maria had said often, when they sat before the campfire at night and she spoke of the many men she had known and married over the years. "He also gave me your mother."

The ring had little value, was a cheap trinket really, yet it had been valued by both of her grandparents, and for that alone, she would keep it.

William had wanted to go to Havers to order a stone marker for the grave. Anastasia had to explain her grandmother's last wishes on the matter.

"My body will rest here, my memory will rest with you, child," Maria had told her that same night she confessed she was dying. "But my name, I wish to keep to myself. If I must rest here, rather than in my own homeland, let there be no evidence of it."

"I will put a marker here someday,"

Anastasia told Sir William. "But it will not bear her name."

Everyone in the camp placed food on the grave that night. It was the duty of the family of the deceased to do so. Dead ones had been known to come and berate their family if this hadn't been done, or so the tales at campfires would relate. This was not the responsibility of friends or mere acquaintances, only family members. Yet everyone in the band honored Maria in this way.

Chapter Twenty-one

"This is going to be so much fun! We can't thank you enough, Will, for thinking of us and letting us share in this endeavor of yours."

Sir William blushed and did a little mumbling that had the three old women giggling to themselves. Anastasia, watching them, hid a smile.

She had heard much about these ladies on the way to London. They were dear friends of William's whom he had known since childhood. Near his age and still quite socially active. His sisters by choice, he fondly called them, and they apparently felt the same way about him.

Victoria Siddons was a widow—for the fourth time, her last husband having left her exceedingly rich and plumply titled, so that for many years she had been one of the more prominent London hostesses, and still was. She entertained frequently in one manner or another, and invitations to her gatherings were quite "the thing" to have.

Rachel Besborough was also a widow, though not so repeatedly as Victoria, having been married to the same marquis for some fifty years before he passed on. She had quite a large family in her children and their offspring, though none still lived with her, so she was more often than not a guest of one of her friends.

Elizabeth Jennings, now, having never married, was quite likely the oldest "old maid" in existence, or so she said with a chuckle about herself. Not that she seemed to mind. She was Rachel's older sister, and so had never lacked having a large family to dote on.

This morning they were all gathered in Lady Victoria's large sitting room in her house on Bennet Street, where William and Anastasia had been staying since they'd arrived in London last week. Anastasia was standing up on a chair, undergoing her second and hopefully last fitting by Victoria's personal seamstress, the wardrobe of fancy gowns that William had promised her almost complete.

Those clothes were all that the ladies were waiting for to "launch" Anastasia on London society. Lady Rachel was keeping a written record, added to daily, of all the fashionable places Anastasia needed to be "seen at." Lady Elizabeth had formed a list of her own, of well-known gossips whom she had already begun visiting.

"Nothing like setting the stage in advance," she had said after returning from her first gossipy visit. "Lady Bascomb is just *dying* to meet you now, gel, and by tomorrow, so will be most of her friends. I swear, she can manage to call upon at least forty different members of the ton in a single day. Do *not* ask me how, but she can."

They had decided a little confusion would be just the thing to spark curiosity, and so each gossip Elizabeth paid a visit to was told something entirely different about Anastasia's history. With her mother supposedly being William's younger sister, who really had run off in her youth and had never returned to England, any and every background they created for Anastasia would be completely plausible.

The three ladies had in fact stayed up very late one night having a great good time designing some pretty outlandish scenarios, from her being the daughter of an illegitimate heir to a throne in Eastern Europe, to the daughter of a rich Turkey slave trader, to the truth, that her father was a Russian Prince. All of which got confided, in absolute secrecy, of course, to the many known gossips on Elizabeth's list.

It became William's task to find out when the marquis arrived in London, and to discover his habits, or at least his normal haunts. After all, this whole scheme was for his benefit, and wouldn't do much good if he didn't hear the gossip, or have a chance to see Anastasia in her new finery.

Once they'd set the scene, the invitations began pouring in. Anastasia, who had yet to make her first "public" appearance, was already in great demand by every hostess in town, thanks to Elizabeth's gossip-spreading talents. Her first appearance, though, would be at the costume party that

Lady Victoria planned for the coming week-end.

Christopher would not be receiving an invite to this. It remained to be seen if he'd show up anyway, to denounce her, just to see what she was up to, or to claim her as his wife. Anything was possible—which was why the ladies were so excited. They could merely set things in motion. They couldn't predict the outcome.

The activity, the in-depth planning, it all helped Anastasia to get beyond the worst of her grief. And she didn't just have the loss of her grandmother and "husband for a night" to deal with, but also of the Gypsies, the people she'd grown up with, people she cared about and who cared about her. She'd said good-bye to them all, though she didn't expect it to be forever. Gypsies never parted for good except in death. They always expected to see old friends and acquaintances again in their travels.

The day of the costume party finally arrived. Anastasia began to feel a certain anticipation, even though she didn't expect to see Christopher tonight, when he had been excluded from the guest list deliberately. After all, it wouldn't do to appear obvious in what they were doing. The whole purpose was to intrigue him, to make him regret her loss, to make him want her back, and to make it easy for him to ignore that "it just isn't done" by showing him just how it *was* done—by keeping the truth to themselves.

Ironically, the first impression she gave to *his* rules-rigid society was that of herself, the truth, because the costume she wore was no costume but her own clothes, her gold dancing outfit. To those gathered, avidly waiting to meet her, she appeared costumed as a Gypsy, and they loved it! She was a smashing success.

Although she did insist on beginning this "farce" with the truth, or a semblance of the truth, she still evaded most questions. The "mystery" is all-important, her new friends had reminded her repeatedly as they prepared for this debut. "Keep them guessing, keep them wondering, never reveal the *real* truth, except in jest."

Which was easy enough to do. Gypsies *were* masters of mystery and evasion, after all, an art she had been raised to know, despite the fact that she had rarely ever made use of such talents before now.

The night went splendidly well, surpassing her friends' expectations. Three quite legitimate, if impulsive, proposals of marriage, eight proposals of a less savory sort, one young man making a complete fool of himself by getting down on his knees in the middle of the dancers to propose to her at the top of his lungs, two other gentlemen coming to blows while vying for her attention.

Christopher didn't show up. Though it had been confirmed that he was in London, they couldn't be sure whether he had heard about her yet. But new gossip would be making the rounds tomorrow. He would hear about her eventually. It was only a matter of time . . .

Chapter Twenty-two

Christopher couldn't manage to get back into the swing of things, now that he had returned to London. He had finished his business at Haverston in haste, then shocked his factor by firing him. Yet he made no effort to find a new factor. He made no effort to do much of anything other than staring into a lot of fires while analyzing the things he should or shouldn't have done concerning Anastasia Stephanoff.

He could *not* get her out of his mind. It had been nearly two weeks since he'd last seen her, yet he could still picture her as if she stood before him. Naked, enraged, under him in bed, the images haunted him like vengeful ghosts that wouldn't go away.

He had gone back to her camp. He had

sworn that he wouldn't, knew that seeing her again would serve no purpose under the circumstances, yet two days after their final parting, he had ridden there again. He wasn't at all sure what he would have said to her at that point, yet he didn't get the chance to find out.

He was incredulous to find the Gypsies gone. He hadn't expected that. Rage quickly followed his amazement, enough that he'd had every intention of sending the law after them. They had claimed his property would be left as they'd found it, after all, yet they had left a grave behind, as well as a large pile of charred wood and metal that indicated one of their wagons had been burned.

Yet he'd no sooner ridden into Havers Town to find the sheriff than his rage was gone. Realizing who that grave might have belonged to was responsible for that. Anastasia's grandmother. And if that was true, then she must be grieving. Oddly, he wanted only to comfort her now. He had to find her first, though.

This he tried to do, sending runners to the closest towns. It was hard to believe they could find no trace whatsoever of the Gypsies. Vanished. Completely. And that was when he began to suspect that he might never see her again.

He was staring into the fire in the parlor at Haverston when he first realized that, and promptly punched a hole in the wall next to the mantel. Walter and David, both there to witness this, wisely said not a word, though they exchanged raised brows.

The next day they returned to London, where his friends quickly abandoned him to his foul mood. He barely noticed their absence, so little had he paid attention to their attempts to cheer him up.

It was their usual habit, though, to prowl one or more of London's many pleasure gardens or spas on a weekend, when they had no specific engagements to attend, and so that first weekend back in London, David and Walter both showed up at Christopher's town house again, to have another go at getting their "old" Kit back.

Some of the gardens could be reached only by river barge, having no land access. The gardens were so popular that many a

Londoner kept a barge for the express purpose of visiting them with friends, rather
than endure a delay in having to rent one.
In their group, David had done the honors,
simply because he owned property on the
river where a barge could be easily docked.

They were fine places of entertainment,
and not just for the aristocracy, but for all
of London. Some, like the New Wells, near
the London Spa, even housed strange ani-
mals, rattlesnakes, imported flying squir-
rels, becoming something of a Zoological
Garden. Some had theaters. Most all had
restaurants, coffee shops, or teahouses, ar-
bors, shaded lanes, vendors, music and
dancing, booths and raffing shops for card-
players and gamblers.

The older of the gardens, Cuper's,
Marybone Gardens, Ranelagh, and Vaux-
hall Gardens, were famed for their evening
concerts, masquerades, and innumerable
illuminations that made them so lovely at
night, and most new gardens were mere
imitations of these four.

For tonight, Walter suggested The
House of Entertainment at Pacras Wells in
northern London. Christopher agreed,

though he couldn't say why, since he simply didn't care one way or the other. However, upon arriving, they went not to see the entertainment, but straight to the Pump Room, where his friends insisted he try the "waters" advertised as being a powerful antidote against rising of the vapors, also against the stone and gravel, and likewise, cleansed the body and sweetened the blood.

He almost laughed. They were obviously going to try any means to bring him out of the brooding he'd fallen into. Not that he believed in natural spring waters, but to humor his friends, who weren't being even the least bit subtle about it, he did drink a bottle, and pocketed a few more to take home with him.

Leaving the Pump Room, they ran into a group of acquaintances, five in number, who, unlike them, *were* actually there for the entertainment. And two of the young men were well-known jokesters, which was probably why David suggested they join the group, hoping they could get a smile out of Christopher, where he and Walter had failed.

He couldn't have known he'd be making matters worse, but that was exactly what happened. And all because one of the young men, Adam Sheffield by name, was in a bad mood himself, but unlike Christopher, he had no qualms about complaining quite loudly about it to his friends. The reason was almost immediately revealed.

"How'm I supposed to meet her if I can't get near her? That old bird is too particular by half, I tell you, in who she invites to her events."

"No need to narrow it down to just her parties, old boy. If you didn't know, she's particular about who she lets into her house at *any* time. Party or no party, you can't just call on Lady Siddons. You have to be an acquaintance, or be with an acquaintance."

"As if she ain't acquainted with just about everyone, old as she is."

"We should have just crashed that silly party," another of them said. "I hear it was in costume. Who would have known the difference, with a few more Pans and Cupids running about the place?"

"Think I didn't try?" Adam told his friend. "Why d'you think I was late joining you? But they were taking bloody head counts *and* names at the door."

"I heard her father was a famous matador," another of the group said now, which got the rest of them contributing to the discussion.

"A what?"

"You know, those Spaniards who actually—"

"Not even close," was said with a hearty laugh. "He's the king of Bulgaria."

"Never heard of it."

"As if that matters—"

"You're both wrong. He's not a king, but a prince, and one from some country where just about everyone's surname has an 'off' in it. Means 'son of,' or daughter in the case of the Stephanoff chit."

"Doesn't matter who her father is," someone else pointed out. "Long as her mother's from good English stock, which I've heard on good authority she is, being that her mother was Sir William Thompson's sister."

"So the chit is Thompson's niece?"

"Yes."

"Well, then, that explains why Lady Siddons has taken his niece under her wing. Sir William has been a neighbor of hers for several centuries."

"They're not *that* old, you dolt. 'Sides, how would you know? You don't run in those circles."

"No, but m'mother certainly does. Who do you think told me that Anastasia Stephanoff was going to be *the* catch of the season? M'mother almost ordered me to put in my bid for the gel."

"When no one's even met her yet? And why is that? Why keep her under such tight wraps?"

"She might be a guest of Lady Siddons, but that doesn't mean she's been hidden away until her launch tonight. Just means we don't know anyone who *has* met her yet."

"Well, half the bloody ton's meeting her tonight," another complained. "Why d'you think Adam's so put out, since *he* didn't get invited."

"Hardly half the ton." This was said dryly, if a touch resentfully. "Pro'bly just those with deep pockets, which don't include us."

"Speak for yourself, old boy," the oldest in the group said smugly. "My pockets are deep enough to suit any would-be husband hunter, but I didn't get invited either. But I'll tell you, Adam, if she's as pretty as I've heard she is, I might just ask for her m'self. Been thinking it's about time to settle down. Actually, m'father's been doing that thinking for me, if you get my drift."

"How do you know she's pretty?"

"Would she be the topic on everyone's mind if she wasn't?" one of them chuckled.

"That hardly signifies. Doesn't take a beauty to become *the* topic."

"Actually, m'oldest sister heard it from Lady Jennings, who's a dear friend of Lady Siddons, that the Stephanoff chit is uniquely beautiful, sort of a cross between a Spanish Madonna and a wanton Gypsy. Just the thing to intrigue a man, if you ask me."

The conversation continued in the same vein as the young bloods approached the theater, but Christopher slowly came to a halt. It took David and Walter a few moments to realize they'd left him behind. Returning to him, it wasn't hard to see that joining that group hadn't been such a good idea after all. His expression bordered on the furious.

"It was that mention that the chit they were talking about looks like a Gypsy," David guessed with a grimace. "What rotten luck."

But Walter said in a reasonable tone, "You know, Kit, you've refused to talk to us about that Gypsy of yours, why she left you when you'd offered to keep her in fine style, why you've been so angry about it. What are friends for, if not to hash things out with?"

"I never even told you her full name, did I?" Christopher said.

David, coming up with pretty good guesses tonight, exclaimed, "Good God, you're not going to say her name's Anastasia Stephanoff, are you?"

"The same."

"But you can't think . . . ?"

"Not bloody likely." Christopher snorted.

"Then don't let it bother you, Kit, if it's

no more than a coincidence, that the two women share the same name," Walter suggested.

"A damned strange coincidence," Christopher replied, his original scowl a bit more pronounced. "Especially considering it's not a name that is even remotely common to England. Besides, I just don't like coincidences that happen to be *that* coincidental."

"Don't blame you a'tall. Definitely strange. But let's get back to your Anna," Walter tried again. "Why did she leave you?"

Walter was pushing it. If Christopher had wanted to discuss his Gypsy with them, he would have done so before now. Yet considering the flaming jealousy he'd just experienced, when he *knew* those young men weren't even talking about his Anna, well, he obviously did need to talk about it, if only to get his mind off of that other girl, who was running around with his Anna's name.

So he said curtly, "Because she objected to my thinking *and* saying she was my mistress."

"Thinking?" David latched on to that word. "I know you got quite foxed the day before. Did you forget to square away the formalities and ask her?"

"No, I did some asking, but apparently not what I'd intended to ask," Christopher mumbled. "Seems instead of making her my mistress, I made her my wife."

Their identical shocked expressions merely confirmed why he should have kept this to himself. A man in his position just didn't make such appalling blunders.

David was the first to recover from his surprise. But he didn't point out the obvious, which Christopher wouldn't have appreciated, having said it enough times himself. *Everyone* knew what he'd done just wasn't done.

And his tone was deliberately calm as he said, "Well, that proves Thompson's niece really isn't the same girl, just in case we were doubting it a'tall. Your wife wouldn't be launching herself in the tried-and-true husband-hunting fashion, now would she?"

Walter rolled his eyes at that reasoning, but what he wanted to know was, "How does one get so drunk that they don't recall getting married?"

"By drinking *too* much, obviously," Christopher replied in self-disgust.

"I suppose," Walter allowed. "But of course, you've rectified the situation?"

"Not yet," Christopher mumbled so softly, he barely heard himself.

Walter certainly missed it, and rather than take the hint that Christopher obviously didn't want to answer, he asked for clarification. "What was that?"

"I said not yet!"

The explosive answer still didn't stop his next question, "Whyever not?"

"Damned if I know." Christopher scowled.

David and Walter exchanged knowing looks at that point, but it was David who expressed their thoughts with, "Then perhaps we should hope that, for whatever strange reason she might have been in that Gypsy camp, your 'wife' and Sir William's niece are one and the same, after all. I'd make a call at the Siddons household tomorrow, indeed I would, were I you,

Kit. Be nice if you were pleasantly surprised."

Would it? Christopher wasn't so sure, but he'd already decided to do just that.

Chapter Twenty-three

Christopher wasn't expecting to be surprised as he was shown into Lady Siddons's parlor, where her "guest" was holding court. Sir William's niece could be a raving beauty as the rumors indicated, but she wouldn't be the Anastasia he was looking for.

After giving it some thought, though, he didn't think the identical names were so coincidental. That would be too far-fetched. It was much more likely that his Anastasia hadn't given him her true name, that she'd met William's niece at some time in the past, liked her name, and decided to take it for her own as well.

Yet he had to find out for sure, thus his early morning visit to old Lady Siddons's house. And not expecting to be surprised just made his surprise all the worse when he saw Anastasia.

She was standing in the center of seven slavering men, all vying for her attention, wearing a morning dress that would have done a queen proud, wide-skirted, tightly corseted, her wild hair caged in a fashionable manner, frilled and laced. Black lace and powder blue satin, making her cobalt blue eyes so incredibly vivid.

For the first startled moment, Christopher actually thought there was merely a resemblance between the two women, so much did she look like an English lady, rather than the Gypsy he had first met. But only for a moment . . .

Their eyes met across the room. She immediately went very still. Then she blushed and lowered her gaze, as if she had something to be guilty about. But then she did, didn't she? Masquerading as a lady. Presenting herself on the marriage mart, when she was already married.

He was letting his jealousy supersede his delight in finding her again. He realized it, and yet those nasty emotions were too powerful to easily ignore, and were coloring his every thought. Even Adam Sheffield was here, obviously having had no trouble getting past the front door this morning, and looking utterly bedazzled by Anastasia. His friend, too, the one who'd mentioned putting a bid in for her himself, was gazing at her worshipfully.

Christopher had the distinctly violent urge to walk over there and knock their heads together, the whole lot of them. How dare they fawn over his wife and entertain lurid thoughts about her? And he had no doubt whatsoever that their thoughts were lurid.

A cross between a Madonna and a wanton, as had been noted last night, was apt by far. Anastasia exuded sexual prom-ise, and yet seemed untouchable, a com-bination ripe for stirring a man's desire, yet making him hesitant to proceed, thus leav-ing him wishful and fantasizing.

Those who were doing no more than fantasizing, he would merely hurt. The oth-ers, though, and he could see there were several others who were actually entertain-ing thoughts of a more permanent nature, unaware that the lady was unavailable for anything permanent, Christopher was going to slowly take apart piece by piece . . .

"I am surprised to see you here, Lord Malory," was said by his side.

He hadn't noticed the dowager countess approaching him. He knew her by sight but couldn't recall ever actually speaking to her before. She, apparently, knew him by sight as well, to know who he was.

As for her wondering at his presence, he replied skeptically, "I doubt that, Lady Siddons, considering who your houseguest is."

"No, truly," she insisted, though she said it with a smile that merely confirmed his impression. "After all, you were privileged enough to obtain the gem, yet foolishly tossed it away."

"I've tossed away nothing, madame," he said stiffly, well aware what she meant, and continuing in the same vein, "The gem is still legally mine."

Her brow shot up, indicating he might have actually surprised her this time, yet her tone was merely curious. "I find that passing strange, considering the connections available to a marquis that would ex-

pedite the disposal of matters of that nature. Perhaps you have merely been delayed in seeing it accomplished?"

"Perhaps I have no intention of doing
anything of the sort," he shot back.

"Well now, that presents a dilemma. It
might behoove you to make the gel aware
of it, since she is quite under a different
impression. Or do you think she's been
launched just to gain your attention?"

"Actually, that she's been launched a'tall
is beyond comprehension," he told her. "Or
aren't you aware of who she really is?"

"Who she is? You mean aside from being your wife?" she rubbed it in, then, "I
can't imagine what you're thinking. She's
my dear friend's niece, of course. I don't
believe you've made his acquaintance.
Well, come along, my lord, and we shall
rectify that."

She walked off, fully expecting him to
follow her. He did, since he did in fact have
a few pertinent questions to put to Sir William Thompson.

The old man was alone, standing sen-
tinel next to a rather large fireplace, where
he'd been keeping a "paternal" eye on his

young "relative." Making quick work of the introductions, Lady Siddons left them alone there.

Christopher didn't mince words, asking right off, "Why have you claimed Anastasia as your niece?"

William didn't answer immediately. He glanced away from Christopher to stare again at the large group in the center of the room, his expression thoughtful. He took a sip from the cup of tea he held.

Christopher didn't get the impression that he was grappling to find an answer. He suspected he was being kept waiting deliberately. To prod his impatience? To punish him? No, that was too ulterior. Perhaps the old man simply hadn't heard him, a distinct possibility considering his age, which was likely in the seventies.

But then Sir William said in a mild tone that could have been discussing any mundane thing, rather than what was likely painful memories, "My sister disappeared some forty-two years ago, Lord Malory. I never forgave myself, at least not until very recently, for my part in it, for not taking her side when she fought with my parents over whom she was to marry. She chose to run away, rather than accept their choice for her, and we never saw her again, nor ever heard from her again. She had lovely black hair, you know. It's not inconceivable that Anastasia could be her daughter, not hard to believe a'tall, actually."

"But she's not, is she?"

William glanced at him again now. He seemed somewhat amused when he said, "Does it matter? When the society that you allow to dictate your actions thinks she is? You want to hear facts, my lord?"

"That would be wonderfully helpful," Christopher said dryly.

Sir William smiled at his tone. "Very well, it's a fact that I was traveling with those Gypsies myself. The reason isn't important, but I was in that camp when you arrived to tell them to leave. You wouldn't have noticed me, though. The truth is, you noticed nothing and no one else, once you set eyes on the lass."

The heated flush came swiftly, the truth of those words embarrassing, though undeniable. "She's uncommonly attractive," Christopher said in his defense.

"Oh, she is that, indeed, but what has that to do with anything, my lord? No, you have only to consider. There is love that takes a long while to grow, then there is love that is immediate. I never wondered at your interest in the lass. It was blatantly apparent."

Love her? Christopher started to snort, then nearly choked on his own derision. Good God, why hadn't he considered that? He had thought he was obsessed with her. He'd thought he was losing control of his own emotions. He'd thought he was letting lust get the better of him. Yet thinking back on it, he recalled how incredibly happy he'd been, waking up to find Anastasia in his bed that morning. He hadn't thought that he might be in love.

"The question, Lord Malory," William continued, "is what are you going to do about it?"

Chapter Twenty-four

He'd come to her. Anastasia hadn't had to go out and be "seen" in places that Christopher might frequent, hoping to run into him. It wasn't going to take weeks, as she'd suspected it would. He'd come to her, and the very next day after her official "launching."

She shouldn't read anything into it, other than that Elizabeth's prior rumor-spreading had paid off, yet Anastasia couldn't help doing so. He was here, and so soon. And she discounted that he was staring green daggers at her. She had expected him to seriously disapprove of what she'd done, considering how he felt about commoners and nobles mixing socially, let alone more permanently.

She was doing a bit more than that,

she was pretending to be something she wasn't, not her idea, but she certainly hadn't balked at it. It would be in line with Christopher's rigid beliefs to denounce her for it. But he didn't, at least not immediately. He spoke with Victoria. Now he was speaking with William. And all the while she was kept in suspense, waiting to see what he would do.

It was impossible to continue to carry on conversations with her admirers when her heart was slamming in anticipation, when her every thought was centered on the large, handsome man across the room, rather than on what was being said to her. If she'd said one word since he walked into the room, she'd certainly never recall it.

She was about to excuse herself and approach Christopher, unable to wait a moment longer when her future happiness was at stake here. But she didn't have to. He began walking directly to her, and his expression had only changed slightly. It was decidedly determined, implacable, and somewhat menacing, a combination that didn't bode too well for Anastasia's hopes.

She held her breath. It wasn't hard to

tell that her attention was utterly transfixed, which had the men around her all glancing toward Christopher as well.

She anticipated an embarrassing scene at that point. What she didn't expect was a very calm, "You'll have to excuse Anastasia, gentlemen. I have a matter to discuss with her that requires privacy."

That, of course, was not met with agreeably, considering the men around her had been almost fighting to retain her attention. It was Adam Sheffield who pretty much summed up, or tried to sum up, their general reaction with, "Now see here, Malory, you can't just—"

Christopher cut that off curtly. "Can't I? Beg to differ, dear boy. A husband has rather pertinent rights, some of which even come in quite handy."

"Husband?"

That was twice more repeated in the shocked silence Christopher left behind him. He didn't stay to elaborate, had no intention of explaining himself. He simply took Anastasia's hand and led her out of the parlor.

She was too shocked herself to have

protested, not that she wanted to protest. He stopped out in the hall to merely say, "Your room will do, lead on."

She did, up the stairs, down another hall, another, then one more. It was a large house. He said nothing else on the way. She was too nervous to speak herself.

Her room was cluttered. The maids didn't get that far in their cleaning until the afternoon. The bed was unmade. The dancing costume she had worn last night was draped over a chair. Several of her new gowns covered another chair—she'd had trouble deciding what to wear this morning, not used to all her choices being so fancy.

He took a moment to survey the room, after closing the door. His eyes *would* linger on that bright gold skirt with the bangled hem. When his glance came back to her, it was distinctly questioning.

"I wore it last night at Victoria's masquerade," she explained.

"Did you? How—apropos."

His tone was just too dry for her frazzled nerves, making her reply stiffly, "Wasn't it? Nothing like presenting the truth and having no one believe it. But then most fools are made, they aren't grown."

He actually chuckled. "How true, and something I've become rather adept at myself lately."

"Making fools?"

"No."

With that simple answer, the stiffness went out of her, leaving only the nervousness. And she wasn't going to ask how he thought he'd made a fool of himself. She could name several times that *she* felt he had, but wouldn't.

Instead, she suggested reasonably, "Shall we discuss why you're here?"

"You mean you weren't expecting me, after launching yourself among the very people I socialize with?" He accepted her blush in answer, but still explained, "I'd heard the niece of a nobleman was calling herself by your name. I came here to find out why. Imagine my surprise . . ."

She had expected his surprise, and his anger. She'd seen the anger, but it wasn't present at the moment. Why it wasn't was what concerned her.

So she asked pointedly, "Why aren't you angry?"

"What makes you think I'm not?"

"You conceal it well, *Gajo.* Very well, what exactly have I done that you object to? Present myself as a lady when you feel I don't have that right?"

"Actually, what I'd like to know is why you've taken on this identity that isn't yours."

"It was not my idea to do, Christoph. I was hurt and angry enough to go about my way, never to see you again. But my grandmother—"

"Your grandmother," he cut in. "I saw the grave, Anna. Was it hers?"

"Yes."

"I'm sorry."

"There is no need to be. It was her time to go, and she was pleased to rest there in that lovely clearing of yours within sight of a road—symbolic of a Gypsy's existence. The worst of my grief is gone. She had long suffered with pain, you see, which made her welcome an end to it, so I can't begrudge her that."

"I'll put a marker—"

"No," she cut in now. "No, it was her wish to keep her name to herself, to have no evidence of it left behind. But as I was saying, Christoph, she still insisted you and I were fated to be. And William, who was traveling with us and heard her, thought you might benefit by being shown that appearances and origins don't mean that much, that—other things—are more important."

"Other things?"

She was not going to spell it out for him, so she shrugged. "To each his own. Some think power is the most important thing in life, some think wealth, some might say happiness, some might say—well, as I said, to each his own."

"You were going to mention love, weren't you?" he asked casually. "Isn't that what you feel is most important in one's life?"

She stared at him hard. He could be mocking her, but she didn't think so.

"No, love by itself is not enough. You can love and be miserable." Something she had been sure she was going to find out firsthand, but she refrained from saying so, merely added, "Love and happiness is what is most important. If they go hand in hand, there is no need to ask for more. But to get both, love must be given and returned."

"I agree."

Those two simple words started her heart slamming again. Yet she was reading too much into it. He might have claimed her in front of those men downstairs, might have given the impression that he was her husband, but of course, it was merely an impression. He hadn't told them that he was her husband, merely mentioned a "husband's rights." Cleverly done, and easy enough to back out of—unless he really *had* intended to make the claim in such a public manner . . .

She knew she was leaving herself wide open for devastation, yet couldn't seem to help it, wanting, needing, clarification. "What—do you agree with?"

"That love must be returned if given, for happiness to occur."

"But this is not what you, personally, consider most important, is it?"

"When my life was empty, or 'something was seriously lacking' in it, as you so aptly put it, I had no idea what that something could be any more than you did."

"I knew," she said softly.

"Did you? Yes, I suppose you did, and simply telling me what it was would have been met with skepticism at that point, as you probably realized."

"At that point?"

He smiled. "If a foolish man is lucky, he remains the fool for only so long, Anna, before he sees how to redeem himself and does so—if it isn't too late. I thought it might be too late, which is why I'm so grateful to Sir William."

"Grateful? For making me acceptable in your social circles?"

"No, for making it possible for me to find you again. I *have* tried, you know. I still have men out searching for your caravan."

"Why?" she asked breathlessly.

He came closer, stopped in front of her, lifted her chin. "For the same reason I have no intention of divorcing you. I want you in my life, Anna, any way I can have you. I know that now. It just took me a few days to realize that marriage, with its permanence, is indeed preferable. The scandal is so very insignificant in comparison."

She wrapped her arms around his neck. What she felt was in her eyes, which drew his lips to hers. There was no passion in his kiss, just a wealth of love and tenderness that sealed their fate more thoroughly than any words could.

Chapter Twenty-five

Christopher took Anastasia straight-away to his London town house, but they didn't stay there long. Within the week he ordered his servants to pack up all of his personal belongings to be moved to Haverston. Much as he might prefer city life, he quickly realized that his wife didn't, and he was much more concerned with making up for what a complete ass he'd been, about the matter of their marriage, than he was with his preferences at the moment.

He would have taken her to Ryding instead. At least it was a much more cheerful house. But she had expressed a desire to be near her grandmother, and so to Haverston they went. He had, of course, remarked on the dourness of the place, to which she'd laughed and told him that could be easily corrected.

"I will hire an army of laborers," he promised her. "It won't take much time a'tall to make that mausoleum habitable, I suppose."

"You'll do no such thing," she told him. "We will effect the improvements ourselves, so that when it's finished, it will be *our* home."

Wield a paintbrush himself? Hold a hammer? Christopher was beginning to realize already just how much his Gypsy was going to change his life. And he was looking forward to every bit of it.

Chapter Twenty-six

It was their first Christmas at Haverston. Christopher had always spent the holidays in London—after all, it was a prime social season. He had no desire to this year. Actually, he had no desire to return to London for any reason. Everything he wanted, everything he loved, was at Haverston.

The house was coming along splendidly, though it was far from finished, since they'd had to slow down their remodeling when Anastasia became pregnant. The main rooms were done, however, and now held a cheerful warmth that had nothing to do with the season, though it was nicely decorated for the season as well.

For Anastasia, it was her first English Christmas as well, and so a new, wonderful experience for her. For her people, Christmas had always been a time to visit as many towns as possible, as quickly as possible because it was a time people spent money on gifts, rather than just themselves, and the Gypsies had many gifts to offer. But that meant they were never in a place long enough to give it a festive look, to decorate a tree, or hang a wreath. That was a *Gajo* thing to do. But not for Anastasia—not anymore.

With her servants to help her, she had unpacked the many trunks that Christopher had had sent from Ryding, filled with Christmas heirlooms that had been in his family for generations, and they had spread them throughout the house together. He hung mistletoe in *every* room, and made the silliest excuses, to lure her under it every chance he got.

She made or bought gifts for all the servants. They delivered them on Christmas Eve, where she got to experience her first sleigh ride, since it had begun snowing earlier in the week, and a thick coat of snow now covered the fields and roads. It was quite fun, despite the cold, and they weren't gone long, since many of the servants lived in the mansion, but the warm parlor was a welcome respite when they returned home.

They spent the rest of the evening there, sitting on the sofa near the fire where a large Yule log burned, watching the small candles flickering on the tree Christopher had gone out and cut down himself.

Anastasia was feeling such peace, such contentment, despite the feeling that had come to her a few days ago that she must try and explain to her husband. It was different from her normal "gift," her insight, and yet it wasn't.

She was four months into her pregnancy. She wasn't actually showing it yet, nor feeling it, other than the brief bouts of sickness she'd had in the mornings for a while. Yet she felt a closeness to her unborn child that was akin to holding him in her arms already. And the feeling that had come to her had to do with him, yet not exactly with him.

It would be best if she could get it into words that made sense, and she tried to do that now, telling Christopher, "There will be one more gift for us to make, though it won't be for us to deliver."

He had one arm around her. His other hand had been idly caressing her arm. He turned to her now to say, not unexpected, "I don't understand." "Neither do I, really," she was forced to admit. "It is just a feeling that has come to me about our son—"

"Son?" he interrupted in surprise. "We're having a son? You actually know this?"

"Well, yes, I had a dream about him. My dreams are usually quite accurate. But that has nothing to do with the gift we must make."

"*What* gift?"

He was starting to sound frustrated. She couldn't blame him. She often questioned herself, the feelings she got.

"We must put down on paper, how we met, how we came to love each other, how we defied our respective people to choose love rather than what was expected of us. We must write our story, Christoph."

"Write it?" He sounded uncomfortable. "I'm not very good with the written word, Anna."

She smiled at him. "You will do fine. I already know this."

He rolled his eyes at her. "I've a better

suggestion. Why don't *you* do this writing that must be done—and by the by, *why* must it be done?"

"We must do this, not for our son, but for his children, and their children. What I have 'felt' is that our story will benefit one or more of these children. I don't know when it will be of benefit, or why, I just know that it will. Perhaps I will know more about it at some future time, have other feelings about it, but just now, this is all I know."

"Very well, I can accept that—I suppose. Yet I still don't see why we both must do this. It only takes one person to tell a story."

"True, except I can't write about *your* feelings, Christoph. I can't write about *your* thoughts. Only you can add these, to make our story complete. But if your style of writing bothers you this much, or if you've had thoughts you think I might question or tease you about, I will promise not to read what you write. This story is not for us, nor for our son, it's for those who will come after, that we will likely never meet. We can lock it away, so no one that we know will ever see it."

He sighed, then kissed her gently on the cheek to make his reluctant acquiescence a tad more graceful. "When do you want to begin?"

She hesitated for only a moment. "Tonight, on Christmas Eve. I have a feeling—"

"No more 'feelings' tonight," he cut in with a moan.

She chuckled. "I didn't say we have to write a *lot* tonight, just a beginning. Besides, I have another gift to deliver tonight that will take quite some time—in the delivering of it."

It was the sensual look she was giving him that had him raising his brow with interest. "You do? Quite some time, eh? You, ah, wouldn't consider delivering that present first, would you?"

"I could be persuaded to."

His lips came to her cheek again, and then moved down her neck, sending shivers over her shoulders. "I'm very good at persuading," he said in a husky whisper.

"I had a feeling you would say that."

Chapter Twenty-seven

Amy closed the journal for the last time with a satisfied sigh. It had been more than she could have hoped for. She was now fully at peace with her "gift." It *could* just be incredible coincidence, how lucky she was with her wagering, but she preferred to think she had inherited her luck from her great-grandmother.

Not everyone had stayed for the full reading, which had taken three days. Roslynn and Kelsey took turns seeing to the children, so they only heard every other chapter or so, though they would catch up, now that they could have the journal to themselves.

Amy's older sisters had decided to wait and read it at their leisure. Though they did pop in every so often to find out how the story was progressing, they mostly kept Georgina company, who was entertaining her visiting brothers elsewhere in the house. The rest of the Andersons didn't come to England frequently enough to suit her, so when they did, she liked to spend as much time as possible with them.

James and Tony, those rogues, had interrupted repeatedly with droll comments about Christopher Malory, whom they had immediately likened to Jason. Jason had sat through the entire reading in pensive silence, not even bothering to scold his younger brothers for their drollery.

Amy's mother Charlotte had been unable to sit for such long periods, and so like her other daughters, she decided to read the journal some other time. But her father, Edward, had stayed for all of the readings, and now came to kiss her brow before he took himself off to bed.

"I don't look like her, as you do," he told Amy. "But like you, I used to wonder why I was always such a good judge of people. That 'insight,' if you want to call it that, is what has aided my investments and made this family incredibly rich. But never being *wrong* makes one feel deuced unusual, indeed it does. Glad to know I'm not the only *strange* one. Indeed, much nicer to know there's a good reason why we've been so fortunate in our many endeavors."

Amy was amazed. Her father might have been the most jovial and gregarious in the family, but he was also the most pragmatic and realistic. She would have thought he'd be the last one to believe in a Gypsy's gift.

Reggie, the only one close enough to have heard Edward's quiet remarks to his daughter, said with a grin, "Don't count yourself short, Uncle Edward. It still takes a certain genius to build the financial empire that you have. Being able to accurately judge the people you invest with helps, certainly, but you still did the picking and choosing. Now, look at me. Like Amy, I took after her in looks, yet I didn't inherit any of these other gifts."

Edward chuckled at her. "I don't mind sharing the credit, puss. And don't be too sure you didn't inherit any gifts. Gypsy charm works its own magic. And have you yet to be wrong in any of your matchmaking endeavors?"

Reggie blinked. "Well, no, come to think of it, I haven't." And then she beamed. "Oh, just wait till I tell Nicholas that he never stood a chance, once I decided to matchmake myself to him."

Reggie's husband had gone to bed several hours ago, simply too tired to stay up to hear the "ending." But the others in the room heard her delighted remark and started commenting, some with humor, some quite appalled . . .

Like Travis, who quickly said, "Just keep those matchmaking tendencies of yours away from me, cousin. I'm not ready to wear the shackles just yet."

"I am," Marshall said, smiling at her. "So do feel quite free to make me your next project."

"Never really thought of it before, but the dear puss really has had quite a hand in matchmaking a lot of us, myself included," Anthony put in. "She did fill my Roslynn's pretty head with nothing but good things about me, expounding on all my good qualities."

"That must have been bloody hard to do," James remarked dryly. "Considering how few good qualities you possess, old man."

"Look who's talking." Anthony snorted. "Can't imagine what George ever saw in you. But then she *has* come to her senses, hasn't she?"

That was hitting rather low, considering it was quite a raw spot for James at the moment, that Georgina still wouldn't talk to him about what was really bothering her, and their bedroom door was still being locked tight against him—especially since Anthony was having no such extended difficulties with his own wife.

So it wasn't the least bit surprising that James replied, albeit with his usual lack of expression, "That black eye of yours is starting to fade, brother. Remind me to rectify that in the morning."

"Not bloody likely. I'll be catching up on quite a bit of lost sleep tomorrow, if it's all the same to you," Anthony retorted.

James merely smiled. "It's not. And do be assured that I can wait until you've caught up. Wouldn't want you in less than top form."

Chagrined, Anthony mumbled, "You're all heart, you bloody ass."

"I'd prefer you two did *not* go at it again," Jason said as he stood up to take himself off to bed. "Sets a bad example for the children."

"Quite right," Anthony agreed with a grin, then to James, "At least *some* of the elders around here are possessed of wisdom."

Considering James was Anthony's elder by a year, there was little doubt that Anthony was getting in yet another subtle dig against him. James might have let it pass if his mood hadn't gone sour with the reminder that his wife was still annoyed with him.

"Which is fortunate," James said, giving his brother a sage nod. "Since some of the *infants* around here are possessed of none a'tall."

Derek, standing next to his father and seeing one of his stern frowns forming, whispered aside to him, "You know once they get started like that, there's no stopping them. Might as well ignore them. I get the feeling it's going to continue like this until Aunt George is smiling again."

Jason sighed and replied in an equally soft whisper, "I suppose I should have a talk with her. From what I've heard, her anger seems quite overdone."

"It does, don't it? Seems to indicate there might be something else that's put the bee in her bonnet, that she ain't fessing up to."

"You've hit the nail squarely. But James has already come to that conclusion himself—not that it's helped any."

"Obviously, since he still ain't himself. Course, he never is, when he and George are having a tiff."

"Are any of us?"

Derek chuckled, likely remembering some of his own tiffs with Kelsey. "Good point. Deuced hard to analyze the situation when you're knee-deep in the doldrums."

Jason was ready to conclude that that might have been his own problem where Molly was concerned. The logic she had always used on him, while valid, always made him rage inwardly that it *was* valid.

The situation, as it had stood, was frustrating beyond endurance, and who could think clearly mired in such emotional muck? Yet he now had hope, thanks to his grandmother's amazing gift.

Jeremy drew his attention back to the current barb slinging by remarking cheerfully, "Well, this 'baby' is taking himself to bed. At least *I* didn't inherit any sorcery-type silliness with these blue eyes and black hair that I got from the *grand-mère.*"

Derek rolled his eyes at that and said in mild disgust, "No, you just cast the most potent spell of all, cousin, in having every woman who looks at you fall hopelessly in love with you."

Jeremy beamed. "I do? Well, hell's bells, I'll settle for that."

Anthony chuckled, putting an arm around Jeremy's shoulders to confide, "They're just jealous, puppy, that all the charm in this family fell on us black-haired Gypsies."

"What rubbish." James snorted. "You've about as much charm as the backside of my—"

Jason cleared his throat very loudly. "I

think we've all been up far too long today,"
he said, and then sternly, "Go to bed, the
lot of you."

"Would if I *had* a bloody bed to go to,"
James mumbled on his way out the door.

Anthony frowned and did some mumbling of his own. "Can't believe I'm feeling
sorry for him. Gads, I must be exhausted.
G'night, all."

Jason looked at Edward and shook his
head with a "what can you do?" sigh, then
turned to Amy to ask, "Do you need help,
m'dear?" He indicated Warren, who was
fast asleep with his head on her shoulder.

She smiled lovingly at her husband.
"No, he wakes very easily."

She shrugged her shoulder to demon-
strate, and Warren sat right up, blinked
once, then said, "All done for the night,
sweetheart?"

"All done for good," she replied, and
handed the journal to Jason for safekeep-
ing. "I'll tell you in the morning what you
missed."

He yawned, stood up, and pulled her to
his side. "I'll let you know, by the time we
get upstairs, whether I can wait until morn-

ing or not to hear how they handled those snooping townsfolk."

She moaned a bit, but then chuckled as she put an arm around his waist. "Same way you probably would have. They told them to mind their own bloody business."

"Excellent, the American way," he replied as he walked them out the door.

They left more'n one English groan behind them.

Chapter Twenty-eight

James paused by his wife's bedroom as he did each night, to see if the door would open. Tonight he was annoyed enough not to bother even trying. She'd been utterly unreasonable in her anger, utterly uncommunicative as well, refusing to discuss it. He really was at his wits' end on how to set things right with her, particularly when he hadn't done anything wrong to be setting right.

He needed a miracle to get out of this mess. That thought reminded him of the conversation he'd had with Jason the night the younguns had snuck into the parlor to open The Present. Before Anthony had found him in Jason's study and they'd started their commiserative drinking, James had found Jason there doing some drinking himself.

"I hope you've got more of that on hand, because I could use a full bottle myself," he told his brother when he entered the room.

Jason nodded. "Fetch a glass on the sideboard and start with this one."

James did, then took the seat across from Jason's desk, waiting for him to pour from the near-empty decanter next to him. When he did, he said pointedly, "I know why *I'm* drinking, but why are you?"

Jason didn't answer that, said instead, "James, you confound me. You, out of all of us, have a certain unique finesse in handling women—at least, you always did in the past. Where's it gone to?"

James leaned back in his chair and took a long swill of his brandy before answering, "Easy to handle women when you aren't emotionally involved with them, quite another thing when you love one to distraction. I've used every means I can think of to get George to at least discuss what's bothering her, but George is, well, George, and she won't budge until she's bloody well ready to. It's got nothing to do with Tony or Jack. I've at least narrowed that down. She merely used them as a convenient excuse to explode—at me. I'm the problem, but since I haven't done a single thing out of the ordinary that might have set her temper off, I'm bloody well in the complete dark."

"It sounds like she just hasn't figured out yet how to approach the matter with you, whatever it is. That could be part of the problem, her own frustration in being unable to express it," Jason suggested.

"George? Having trouble expressing herself?" James all but rolled his eyes.

"Not ordinarily," Jason agreed. "But this doesn't sound like an ordinary problem, or it *would* be out in the open already, wouldn't it?"

"Possibly," James allowed thoughtfully, then, "Bloody hell. I'm done with trying to figure out what's wrong. Everything I make a guess at just points out more clearly that this makes no sense a'tall."

Jason, staring at the glass in his hand, snorted. "Women make sense when they're upset? When did they ever?"

James chuckled at that, since it reminded him of the realization he'd come to a few years ago, yet he'd never broached the subject with his brother. It also gave him his answer to why his brother might be in need of a fortifying brandy or two. In a word, women problems.

So he asked baldly, "How long have you been in love with Molly?"

Jason glanced up, but his expression didn't show the surprise that question should have brought. "Since before Derek was born."

James couldn't quite conceal his own surprise at that answer and the obvious conclusion it brought. "Good God . . . well, damn it all, Jason, why the deuce have you never told any of us?"

"You think I didn't want to? I'd shout it from the rooftops if it were my choice, but it's not. Molly had valid reasons for wanting the truth about us kept secret, even from Derek—at least she managed to convince me those reasons were valid. I'm not so sure anymore, but that's a moot point after all these years of secrecy."

"Why don't you just marry the woman

and have done with it?" James said reasonably.

Jason laughed without humor. "I'm *trying* to. I have been trying to since the divorce from Frances, but Molly won't budge in her refusal. She's got this gigantic scandal imagined in her mind and she refuses to inflict it on the family."

James raised a golden brow. "On the family? When has this family *not* had a scandal brewing of one sort or another?"

Jason raised a brow himself. "True, to which you, for one, made sure of."

James chuckled at his brother's censorious tone. "Let's not get into that. I'm reformed, don't you know."

Jason shook his head bemusedly. "I still can't credit how *that* came about."

"Love, of course. It does produce amazing miracles. Speaking of which, it's looking like I'll need one of those to get out of this confounding situation with George. If I find one, Jason, I'll be sure to pass it along, since you seem to be in need of a miracle yourself as well."

Remembering that conversation with his brother, James had a feeling that Jason might have found his miracle, thanks to their grandmother, yet one hadn't dropped into his own lap yet. But enough was enough and tomorrow he'd tell his wife so. Tonight he was simply too tired. Tonight he'd probably say something he'd end up regretting, and then he *would* have something to apologize for.

He walked away, but no more than three steps were taken before he spun about and pounded on her door. To hell with waiting. He was tired, yes, but he was even more tired of sleeping alone.

From inside the room he heard, "It's open."

James frowned down at the doorknob, tried it. Damned if it wasn't open. Bloody hell. It would have to be open the one time he made a racket pounding on it rather than just checking it first.

He entered the room, closed the door, then leaned back against it, crossing his thick arms over his chest. Georgina was sitting on the bed, wearing the white silk negligee and robe that he'd given her last Christmas. She was brushing her long brown hair. He always enjoyed watching

her do that—another thing he'd been denied lately.

He raised a brow at her and asked dryly,
"Forget to lock the door?"

"No," she said simply.

The golden brow lifted just a bit higher.
"Don't tell me you've gotten all maudlin
over the elders' love story and decided to
forgive me because of it?"

Her sigh was loud enough to hear
across the room. "Maudlin, no. Finally realizing that putting this off isn't going to
make it go away, yes, their story did help
me to see that the unavoidable can't be
avoided. So you may as well know, there's
nothing to forgive you for, James."

"Well, I always knew that, but what the
devil d'*you* mean by nothing?"

She lowered her gaze and mumbled
something that he couldn't make out. This
had him crossing the room to stand in front
of her. He lifted her chin. Her large brown
eyes were inscrutable. She'd learned how
to do that from him.

"Let's try this again, shall we?" he said.
"Now, what d'you mean, there's nothing to
forgive me for?"

"I was never angry with you. The way I've been behaving had nothing to do with you—well, it did, but not for the reason I let you think. I was already upset about something else when Jack said what she did. I used that as an excuse, because I wasn't ready to fess up to the other. I didn't want to upset you."

"I hope you know, George, that you haven't made one bloody bit of sense. Didn't want to upset me? Do I look like I haven't been upset?"

His frown answered that question quite satisfactorily. She actually smiled.

"Let me rephrase that," she suggested. "I didn't want to upset you with what was really bothering me, which was not wanting to upset you at all."

He made a sound of frustration at that point. "I know it's American reasoning that makes what you say sound like gibberish to the English mind, but do try—"

"Rubbish," she cut in with a snort. "I'm just still hedging, is all."

"Good of you to own up to that, m'dear. Now own up to why."

"I was getting to that," she continued to hedge.

"Notice I'm patiently waiting."

"You're never patient."

"I'm *always* patient, and you're *still* hedging," he all but growled. "George, I'm warning you, I'm bloody well at the end of my patience."

"See?"

He gave her a scowl worthy of decimating an ordinary opponent. She was unaffected, well aware she had nothing to worry about from his scowls. But she was pushing it. Finally she sighed again.

"I know you love the twins," she said. "You can't help but love them, they're such darlings. But I also know you were horrified at the thought of having them, when Amy and Warren produced twins, and him being my brother, you realized we might have some, too."

"Not horrified," he corrected. "Just bloody well surprised that they run in your family, when your family didn't have any to show for it."

"Horrified," she reiterated stubbornly.

He sighed this time, though only for effect. "If you insist. And your point?"

"I didn't want to horrify you again."

"Again?" And then he blinked. "Good God, George, are we having another baby?"

At which point she burst into tears. James, on the other hand, burst into laughter. He simply couldn't help it. But that just had her crying louder.

So he lifted her up, sat down on the bed and placed her on his lap, wrapped his arms around her carefully, and said, "You know, George, we're really going to have to work on your way of announcing these things. Recall how you told me about Jack's impending arrival?"

She did indeed. They'd been in the middle of a heated exchange on his ship, where she'd just got done calling James an English *lord,* a Caribbean *pirate!*

He'd replied, "I hate to point this out, you little witch, but those aren't epithets."

She'd shouted back, "They are as far as I'm concerned. My God, and to think I'm going to have your baby."

To which he had countered heatedly,

"The devil you are! I'm not touching you again!"

She had stomped away with the parting shot, "You won't have to, you stupid man!" which had finally got the point across to him that she was already pregnant.

"And the second time, d'you recall that you actually denied you were pregnant? Told me you were just putting on a little weight, as if I couldn't bloody well tell the difference." He snorted.

She stiffened at that point. "You blame me for not mentioning it, after what you said when Amy had her twins? 'We are not having any, d'you hear!' Those were your exact words, you odious man. Well, we did have some, didn't we, and we may have some more, and some more, and—"

"How you do go on," he cut in with a chuckle. "My dearest girl, you shouldn't hold a man accountable for one unguarded moment of surprise."

"Shock," she corrected.

"Surprise," he repeated adamantly. "That's all it was, you know. And I did adjust to it remarkably well, if I do say so myself. In fact, you can give me twins every year if you're up to it, and I'll adore them all equally. You know why, don't you?"

She frowned. "Why?"

"Because I love you, and at the risk of sounding exceedingly conceited," he added with a smug grin, "I know you love me, too. Stands to reason, then, don't it, that anything that we produce from that love will be cherished, whether it comes in a single package or in pairs. I'll love them all, silly girl. Don't ever doubt that again."

She put her head against his chest with a sigh. "I have been rather silly, haven't I?"

"Considering where I've been sleeping lately," he replied dryly, "I'll refrain from answering that, if it's all the same to you."

She kissed his neck in apology. "I'm really sorry about that."

"As you should be."

It was his condescending tone that prompted her to reply, "Did I ever mention that four generations back, there was a rare instance of triplets in my family?"

"I know you're expecting to hear yet another 'Good God, George, we're not having any of *those* either,' but I'm going to have to disappoint you. Now, if I *didn't* think you were pulling my leg . . ."

She giggled, which more or less admitted she was doing just that. But then she asked curiously, since she had come upstairs early, "Did Amy finish the journal tonight?"

"Yes. Amazing gift my grandmother had. I prefer to think it was just incredible good guessing on her part, but who's to say for sure?"

"My, I did miss a lot, didn't I?"

James nodded. "You'll want to read it for yourself, if you can manage to get it away from Jason. I've a feeling he has someone else he'd like to have read it first, though."

"Molly?"

James chuckled. "So you noticed, too?"

"The softening of his edges whenever she's around? Who could miss that?"

"Just *most* of us," he replied dryly.

Chapter Twenty-nine

"Did it get finished tonight?" Molly asked when Jason joined her in her bed that night.

"Sorry, did I wake you?"

She yawned and snuggled up close to him. "No. I've just missed you these last nights, so I tried to stay awake tonight. Didn't think I was going to manage it, though. I was just nodding off."

He smiled and pulled her close. He'd had no chance to talk to her since that journal had been unwrapped. She'd been asleep these last few nights by the time he came to her, and gone in the mornings, she rose so early. Nor, with the house so full, was there much chance to find her alone during the day to have a few private words.

And the subject of the journal wouldn't

be discussed by the rest of the family, at least not in front of the servants, which they all considered Molly to be—with the exception of Derek and his wife, and now James, who knew the truth about her, that she was Derek's mother, that she'd been Jason's only love for more'n thirty years.

So Molly wouldn't know yet what was in the journal. However, she couldn't help but know that the family had all been camped in the parlor for three days, hearing it read. She had appeared in the doorway several times to shake her head over the fact that they were all still there.

"I want you to take the day off tomorrow and read it for yourself," he told her.

"Take the day off? Don't be silly."

"The house will get along fine without you for a day, m'dear."

"It won't."

"Molly," he said warningly.

She mumbled, "Oh, all right. It *could* wait until after the holidays, when the house isn't so full, but I'll admit to a certain curiosity about that journal, after having it in my possession for most of my life, yet not knowing what it was."

He sat up abruptly. "Most of your life? When did you find it? And where?"

"Well, I did—and I didn't. What I mean is, it was given to me when I was but a child of four or five—I can't remember which. I was told what to do with it, and when to deliver it, but not what it was. And I must confess that it was so long ago, Jason, that I put it away with some old things of mine and completely forgot about it ever since. It's been up in your attic all these years, with my old childhood things that I have stored there."

"But you finally remembered it?"

"Well, no, and it was the strangest thing, how I found it again," she admitted.

"What do you mean?"

She frowned to herself, remembering. "It was when I first started fetching the Christmas decorations down from the attic. The sun had been out most of the day, which had caused the attic to be quite stuffy and warm, so I opened one of the windows up there, yet it didn't do much good other than let in a little cold air, since no breeze was stirring, and wouldn't have come into the room anyway, with only the one window open—or so I thought. Yet just when I was heading toward the door with my last load for the day, this great gust of wind tore through the room, knocking things all over the place."

"You'd left the door open, to account for such a strong cross breeze?"

"It was no breeze, Jason, it was a very strong wind, which didn't make much sense to begin with, when it hadn't been a bit windy that day. But no, the door was closed, which is why I found that wind so strange, least I did afterwards, when I had time to think about it. At the time, though, I was too busy picking the things up that it knocked over. It was when I came to this large folding Oriental room divider, that had fallen over on a stack of paintings, jarring several out of their frames, that I noticed my old things. I *still* didn't recall the journal, though, and wouldn't have bothered to look inside that old trunk of mine, except, well . . ."

Her frown got deeper. He almost shook her, to get her to finish.

"Well?" he demanded.

"Well, if the wind didn't gust once more

in that corner, rattling the lid on the trunk something fierce. I swear, it seemed almost as if the wind was trying to open it. It really was the strangest damned thing. Gave me the chills, I don't mind telling you. And *that's* when I remembered that old leather-wrapped thing I'd put in that trunk long before I ever came to Haverston to work—and that I was supposed to give it to your family as a gift. Stranger yet, soon as I did open the trunk, the wind stopped completely."

He laughed suddenly. "I can just hear what Amy would say about that if she'd been there. She'd insist it was my grand-mother's ghost, or perhaps even *her* grand-mother's ghost, making sure the journal got delivered. Good God, don't ever tell her about that wind, Molly. She really will think this old place is haunted."

"Nonsense. It was just a wind, likely stirred up by the heat in the room."

"Yes, obviously, yet my niece is a bit fanciful, so let's keep that part of your dis-covery to ourselves, shall we?" he sug-gested with a smile.

"If you insist."

"Now tell me who gave it to you all

those years ago. You aren't old enough to have known my grandmother."

"No, but my grandmum was. And it all came back to me when I found it again, what she'd told me when she gave the present into my keeping. She'd been Anna Malory's personal maid, you know."

He grinned at her. "Now, how would I have known that, when you never bothered to mention it before?"

She blushed. "Well, I'd forgotten about that, too. I don't remember much about my grandmum, since I was so young when I knew her, and she died soon after she gave me that journal. And my mother never worked here at Haverston, so she'd had no dealings with the Malorys herself, nor ever had reason to mention them, which made it all the easier for me to forget about it. And it was more than ten years later before I came to work here myself, but even that didn't stir my memory."

"So Anna Malory gave it to your grandmother to deliver?"

"No, she gave it to her to give to me. Let me tell you what my grandmum told me, and maybe you'll understand. I certainly didn't at the time, and still don't, but here it is, best as I can remember. My grandmum was already Lady Malory's maid, but the lady summoned her one day, told her to sit and have tea with her, that they were going to be the best of friends. Grandma said the lady often said strange things, and one of them she said that day. She said, 'We're going to be related, you know. It won't be for a very long time, and we won't see it happen, but it will happen, and you'll help it to happen when you give this to your granddaughter.' "

"The journal?"

Molly nodded. "Lady Malory had more to say about it, specific instructions actually. My grandmum admitted she'd thought the lady was daft at the time. After all, she didn't have a granddaughter yet. But the instructions she was given was to have her granddaughter—me; I'm the only one she ever got, after all—deliver the present to the Malory family for Christmas in the first quarter of the new century. Not to any specific member of the family, just to the family. And being a gift, she wanted it to look like a gift. And that's all she had to say about it. No, wait, there was one other thing. About the time of delivery. She said, 'I have the feeling that's when it will be of the most benefit.' "

Jason smiled slowly and gave his grandmother a silent thank-you. To Molly he said, "Amazing."

"You understand it, then?"

"Yes, and so will you, I think, as soon as you read it. But why didn't you leave a note with it, so we would have at least known who it was for, and who it was from? Not knowing turned it into quite a mystery, which is why the younguns didn't wait for Christmas to open it."

"Because it was for all of you, of course." And then she chuckled. "Besides, if it turned out to be nothing important, I wasn't going to own up to putting it there."

"Oh, it was important, sweetheart, and more than that, a valuable heirloom for this family. And I'm most definitely looking forward to hearing what you have to say after you read it."

She gave him a suspicious look. "Why do I get the feeling I'm not going to like whatever's in that journal?"

"Possibly because you're so pigheaded stubborn about certain things."

"Now you're really starting to worry me, Jason Malory," she said in a grumbling tone.

He grinned. "No need to fret, love. Only good things will come of it, I promise."

"Yes, but good for *whom?*"

Chapter Thirty

Christmas morning dawned bright if chilly at Haverston, though the parlor where most of the family was gathered was quite comfy, with a nice fire crackling. Jeremy had lit the small candles on the decorated tree. Though the extra light wasn't needed, the flickering flames fascinated the children, and the sweet scent from the candles was a nice touch.

The last to arrive were James, Georgina, and their three younguns. Jack ran immediately to her oldest brother, Jeremy, whom she adored, and got her usual tickle and hug from him. Then, typically, she headed straight for Judy, ignoring everyone else, though she would make the rounds to greet the rest of her large family after the two young girls finished their morning whisperings.

Anthony, never one to let a prime moment pass, said to his tardy brother, "Now that you've managed to find that bed of yours again, having trouble getting out of it, eh?"

Anthony had got most of his teasing done yesterday, though. When he'd seen James in such obvious good spirits, he'd been unable to resist taunting, "What? No longer in a mood to pass out black eyes?"

"Put a lid on it, puppy," his brother had replied with a snort.

That never worked, at least not with Anthony anyway. "George has forgiven you, I take it?"

"George is having another baby, or babies, as the case may be," James said drolly.

"Now, that's what I call a nice Christmas present, news like that. Congratulations, old boy."

Just now, though, it wasn't James who replied to Anthony's renewed teasing, it was his own wife who, in her charming Scots burr, said, "Put a lid on it, mon, or you'll be wondering where your own bed has gone."

To which James burst out laughing, and Georgina said, "It wasn't *that* funny. Notice your brother isn't one little bit amused."

"Course I did, love, and *that's* what's funny," James replied.

Anthony did some mumbling and shot James a disgusted look before he leaned close to whisper something to his wife that had her smiling. Obviously, notorious charmer that he was, he'd just patched things up nicely.

The present-opening began soon after, with the children all gathered on the rug before the tree. Judy noticed the missing Present on its pedestal, and went to Amy for questioning. She and Jack hadn't come near the parlor during those days the journal was being read, having much more adventurous things to do at their age.

"It was just a book?" Judy asked after Amy answered her first question, obviously disappointed that what had caused her and Jack such interest was actually not at all interesting in her mind.

"Not just a book, love. It tells the story

about your great-grandparents, how they met, how it took them a while to realize that they were meant for each other. You'll want to read it someday."

Judy did not look impressed, and in fact was already distracted, watching Jack open her next present. But several of the adults were close enough to have heard her questions, and reminded of the grandparents they all shared, had a few more comments to make.

Travis said, "I wonder if he ever liked this place, considering how much he hated it at first."

"Course he did, since *she* was in it," his brother replied. "Makes a world of difference if you've someone to share things with."

Anthony commented, "Find it remarkable that he agreed to brighten the place up himself. Wouldn't catch me wielding a bloody hammer."

"No?" his wife said pointedly.

"Well . . . perhaps." Anthony grinned. "Wonderful thing, the proper incentive, specially when it yields wonderful results."

Roslynn rolled her eyes, but it was

Derek who said with a chuckle, "You'll have to admit, they did a good job on fixing the place up. For all its huge size, Haverston still has a homey feel to it."

"Only because it's been *your* home," his wife replied pointedly. "To those not raised here, it has more the feel of a royal palace."

"My thoughts exactly," Georgina agreed.

"American thoughts don't count, George," James told his wife dryly. "After all, we know quite well you won't find such grandeur in those primitive States of yours, barbaric as they still are."

Anthony chuckled at that, nodding across the room to where Warren was sitting on the floor before the Christmas tree with one of his twins on each knee, quite involved with helping them to open their presents. "Wasted that one, old man. The Yank didn't hear you."

"But this Yank did," Georgina replied, giving James a jab in the ribs to show how much she appreciated his disparaging remarks about her country.

He grunted, but it was to Anthony that he replied, "Do be a good chap and remind me to repeat it later, when he is within hearing."

"You may depend upon it," Anthony replied.

They were, after all, united when it came to their nephews-by-marriage, against them, that is, despite their merciless barbs reserved for each other when the "enemy" was not around.

Reggie came by, passing out a few presents, one of which she dropped in James's lap. It was from Warren.

"See if that doesn't change your mind about keeping today, of all days, friendly," she said.

He raised a brow at her, but opening the package, he chuckled. "Hardly, puss," he said, examining a small bronze caricature of an obvious English monarch looking decidedly silly. "Couldn't ask for a nicer gift, though."

Since it was a gift meant to provoke, James *would* be delighted with it. Warren *was* his preferred and most challenging barb-slinging choice, after all, with Reggie's husband coming in a close second.

"Famous," Reggie said, rolling her eyes.

"Though I should be relieved. At least my Nicholas will be spared, now that you have your target for the day."

"Don't count on it, m'dear." James grinned wickedly. "Wouldn't want him to feel neglected just because it's Christmas."

Molly appeared in the doorway just then. Jason hadn't spoken to her since she had started reading the journal. She had finished it late last night, long after he'd gone to bed. He came to her now with a hopeful look, and she knew exactly why he wore it.

But reaching her, he glanced up at the doorframe they stood under. She followed his gaze to see the mistletoe hung there as it was every year. Before it even occurred to her that he might do something outlandish like kiss her with his *entire* family in the room and possibly watching, he kissed her, and quite thoroughly, too.

A few breathless moments later, he said, "Do I need to ask my question—again?"

She smiled, knowing exactly which question he meant. "No, you don't," she whispered, so they wouldn't be overheard.

"And my answer is yes, though with one condition."

"Which is?"

"I'll marry you, Jason, if you'll agree that we won't tell anyone about it, aside from your family, of course."

"Molly—" he began with a sigh.

"No, hear me out. I know that's not what you were hoping I'd say, after reading about your grandparents. But things were different for them. She was a stranger to the area. The people here and in Havers didn't know her most of their lives. It was easy for them to ignore inquiries, or put them off, so that no one ever did really know the truth. But you can't deny that they didn't own up to the truth, that only a select few ever knew—and besides, her father *was* a Russian noble, even if her mother wasn't."

He rolled his eyes. "And your point?"

"You know I can't say the same, Jason. And I still won't bring more scandal on your family, when it's already borne so many scandals in the past. If you can't agree to keep a marriage between us secret, then we'll just have to go on as we have been."

"Then I suppose I'll have to agree to those terms, of course."

She gave him a suspicious look, considering she had been anticipating much more of an argument from him. "You wouldn't agree now, only to change your mind after we're married, would you?"

He feigned a hurt look before asking her, "You don't trust me?"

She scowled. "I *know* you, Jason Malory. You'll do or say just about anything to get your way."

He grinned. "Then you should know that I'd never do anything to get you seriously annoyed with me."

"No, not unless you thought you could talk me around it. Need I remind you that I'd consider this a serious breach of promise?"

"Need I remind you just how happy you've made me, agreeing to be my wife—finally?"

"You're changing the subject, Jason."

"You noticed?"

She sighed. "As long as we understand each other."

"Oh, we do, sweetheart." His smile was so very tender. "We always have."

Behind them, they heard a cough, which reminded them both that they weren't alone. They turned as one to face the room, and found every member of his family staring at them. Molly started blushing. Jason was grinning from ear to ear, and he didn't waste time explaining why.

"Allow me to announce," he said, taking Molly's hand in his, "Molly has given me the greatest Christmas gift I could have asked for in agreeing to be my wife." Which, of course, started everyone talking at once.

"About bloody time," James commented first.

"You can say that again," Derek said, and with a whoop of delight, came forward to hug his parents.

"It's too bad this wasn't settled sooner," Reggie remarked, smiling. "We could have had a Christmas wedding today."

"Who says we can't?" James replied. "I happen to know the elder has had a special license ready and waiting for quite a few years now. And if I know my brother, he isn't going to give Molly a chance to change her mind."

"Goodness! So this didn't just develop?"

Nicholas chuckled at his wife. "Take a good look at Derek and Molly, standing there together, sweetheart. That ought to give you your answer."

Reggie did, then said, "Oh, my. I think Uncle James said it aptly."

And Amy giggled. "He did, didn't he? Of course, I've known for the longest time, having caught them kissing once. I just didn't know it would one day lead to this."

"And to think I had no hand in matchmaking them," Reggie sighed.

James chuckled at his niece. "How could you, when they were in love before you were even born?"

"I realize *that,* but you said it yourself, Uncle James. They've been a bit tardy in getting around to marrying, and I consider it my department to push these sorts of things along."

Anthony laughed at that. "Don't think you could've helped this time, puss. Actually, come to think of it, I'd say it took The Present to do it."

And James said dryly, "You only just figure that out, dear boy?"

Anthony's brow rose, but before he came back with a rejoinder, Charlotte was heard from. "A Christmas wedding, how utterly wonderful. I think I'm going to cry."

"You always cry at weddings, m'dear," Edward said, patting her hand.

That being the first remark from Edward, and hardly what Jason was expecting from his closest brother, particularly since he'd been the one most vocal against his divorce, Jason asked, "No comment about an impending scandal, Edward?"

Edward looked a bit embarrassed as he admitted, "We've muddled through all the other scandals this family has created. I imagine we'll muddle through this one just fine." And then he grinned. "Besides, now that you're finally marrying for the *right* reasons, I couldn't be happier for you."

"There doesn't have to be a scandal," Reggie said. "Or have you all forgotten The Present so soon? I don't see why we can't take a leaf from those old friends of Sir William Thompson's. Gossip is an amazing thing, after all. If so many conflicting things are heard about the latest major on-dit, then no one can really point to the truth and hold it up as fact. No one knows for sure what is the truth, thus what will be believed is what one chooses to believe."

But Molly was shaking her head. "My case isn't the same as your great-grandmother's. People around here knew my father."

"Yes, but did they know his father, or his father before him? For all you know, Molly, you could have a lord or two up your ancestral tree. It's a rare family that doesn't have a few ancestors conceived on the wrong side of the blanket in one century or another."

Derek chuckled at that point and told his mother, "You know once Reggie latches on to an idea, she rarely lets go of it. Might as well let her have her fun with the gossips. After her success in Kelsey's case, she will anyway."

Molly sighed, having had her one stipulation to the wedding, that no one else should know about it, taken out of her hands. Jason, understanding, pulled her closer to his side to say for her ears only, "Remember what my grandfather Christopher had to say on the subject?"

She glanced up at him in surprise, but then she smiled. "Yes, point taken."

"Good. And I hope you've noticed, not one objection from my family."

That reminder got him a poke in the ribs. "Rubbing it in is not allowed. And besides, they aren't objecting because they all love you and want you to be happy."

"No, it's because you've always been part of this family, Molly. We're just going to make it official now—and about bloody time."

About the Author

With more than 54 million copies of her books in print and translated into twelve languages, JOHANNA LINDSEY is one of the world's most popular authors of historical romance. Every one of her previous thirty-two novels has been a national best-seller, with several reaching the #1 spot on the *New York Times* list. Ms. Lindsey lives in Hawaii with her family.